P9-CQA-824

D0015040

ALSO BY DEB CALETTI

*A Flicker of Courage*


FOR OLDER READERS

*Girl, Unframed*
*A Heart in a Body in the World*
*Essential Maps for the Lost*
*The Last Forever*
*The Story of Us*
*Stay*
*The Six Rules of Maybe*
*The Secret Life of Prince Charming*
*The Fortunes of Indigo Skye*
*The Nature of Jade*
*Wild Roses*
*Honey, Baby, Sweetheart*
*The Queen of Everything*

# THE WEIRD in the WILDS

## TALES OF TRIUMPH AND DISASTER!

## DEB CALETTI

putnam

G. P. Putnam's Sons

G. P. PUTNAM'S SONS
An imprint of Penguin Random House LLC, New York

Visit us online at penguinrandomhouse.com

Library of Congress Cataloging-in-Publication Data
Names: Caletti, Deb, author.
Title: The weird in the Wilds / Deb Caletti.
Description: New York: G. P. Putnam's Sons, [2020] | Series: Tales of triumph and disaster! | Audience: Ages 8–12. | Audience: Grades 4–6. | Summary: "When their village's evil leader, Vlad Luxor, turns the class bully into a stinky gerenuk, Henry, Jo, Apollo, and Pirate Girl must once again put their spell-breaking talents to the test on another extraordinary adventure"—Provided by publisher.
Identifiers: LCCN 2019058182 (print) | LCCN 2019058183 (ebook) |
ISBN 9781984813084 (hardcover) | ISBN 9781984813091 (ebook)
Subjects: CYAC: Magic—Fiction. | Friendship—Fiction. | Good and evil—Fiction. | Kings, queens, rulers, etc.—Fiction. | Adventure and adventurers—Fiction.
Classification: LCC PZ7.C127437 We 2020 (print) | LCC PZ7.C127437 (ebook) |
DDC [Fic]—dc23
LC record available at https://lccn.loc.gov/2019058182
LC ebook record available at https://lccn.loc.gov/2019058183

Printed in the United States of America
ISBN 9781984813084

1  3  5  7  9  10  8  6  4  2

Design by Eileen Savage | Text set in Cheltenham ITC Pro

Here's to my beautiful, growing family, and to the way the record keeps spinning, with old songs and new ones.

## CHAPTER 1

# A Dreadful Event

Henry Every has no clue that something terrible and shocking is about to happen. The poor boy will soon get scared out of his wits. You'd think Henry would be on his toes about such possibilities after what occurred just a few weeks ago: the terrifying trip up Rulers Mountain, facing the evil Vlad Luxor, and turning Rocco Dante from a naked lizard back into a child. And now that there's a *new* horrible problem troubling the good people of the Timeless Province . . . well, you'd think he'd be *especially* aware. But Henry's mind is on other things. It's the first day of school. The first day of school is always somewhat nerve-racking, and Henry's a shy boy, so he could barely sleep last night. Right at this moment, his tummy is spinning and thumping like a pair of tennis shoes in the dryer.

It's a chilly and beautiful fall morning, and outside Henry's bedroom window, the trees look like giant orange and red balloons. Leaves spiral in a gust of wind. The season has changed, and other things have changed, too. But unfortunately, a lot hasn't.

"Stop dawdling, Henry! You're a big sloth. You're going to be late for school like you always are!" Henry's mother screeches. Her voice climbs up the stairs and shoots through his body, rattling his spirit.

"And take that stinky, whiny mutt outside," Henry's father shouts. "All she does is bark and jump on the furniture when you're gone."

Henry and his Jack Russell terrier, Button, look at each other. If eyes can sigh, theirs do. Of course, Button *never* jumps on the furniture, and only barks when it's truly necessary and extraordinarily helpful or when a doorbell rings on TV. She smells like any good dog, which means kind of like a soggy wool blanket, but in the nicest way. And of course, Henry has *never* been late for school, and he's not a big anything. He's rather small and skinny and kind. He's quiet and thoughtful, and he always hopes for the best.

Now, thank heavens, Henry finally sees Apollo Dante and the whole Dante family leave their house. Apollo waves at Henry up in his window. It's time, it's time, it's time! Anxiety and excitement smash together like two exploding asteroids on *Rocket Galaxy*. Henry runs downstairs as Button races ahead.

On this day, when other children are wearing their new school clothes, Henry is wearing only old school clothes. His jeans are as thin as a bedsheet, and his bare wrists stick out from his cuffs, and one of his big toes pokes through his tennis shoe like a periscope from a submarine. Henry's backpack is a crinkled grocery bag from the Always Open (now, sadly, named *Vlad's*), and his lunch box is a used athletic sock of his father's, filled with a single boiled potato. He did not go to Cadabra, the Store with Everything, in order to get fresh school supplies for the year. He has *one* school supply, which he found under the couch cushions: the saddest pencil you've ever seen in your life.

*The Saddest Pencil You've
Ever Seen in Your Life*

Henry is nearly at the door when his mother steps in front of him and folds her arms. "What have you forgotten, Henry? What are the three magic words?"

"I—I . . ."

She stares at him hard, waiting. "You what?"

The words feel like a giant, wrinkly apricot pit in his stomach, but he knows what he must do.

"I love you," he manages to whisper, and then his mother huffs and opens the door and lets him pass. Sadly, this is also still the same: the way it's mostly impossible and dangerous for Henry to use his very own voice in a way that's true.

Henry steps into the fall air and runs down the rickety steps of the Every house. Now that he's out in the open, he remembers to cautiously look left and then right. A shiver trickles down his arms, and a prickly awareness goes up his spine, because things are as dire as ever in the world beyond his house, too: Vlad Luxor is still their HRM—Horrible Ruler with Magic—living in that black-mirrored tower on Rulers Mountain, and Mr. Needleman is still his vile right-hand man. The good people of the Timeless Province continue to be constantly afraid, as Vlad Luxor struts around town, staring at his reflection in store windows and mud puddles, and using his power to cast every kind of random, cruel spell. Just last week, he told Professor M. Eritus that she had a horse face and then he turned her into a donkey. He changed their beloved produce man, Mr. Tim Apple, into an actual McIntosh Red for no reason at all, and the poor man nearly got baked into a pie.

But something else has been happening lately as well. A terrible, worrisome new trouble. As if constant fear and utter havoc weren't bad enough, things have recently gotten darker and even *more* evil in the province. It began one day with an unusual message on the blue scrolling banner above Vlad's billboard in the town square, a message about

INNERS and OUTERS, OTHERS and US. And then came more such messages, and more, and more, as if Vlad was a parrot, squawking one awful thing over and over. On that sign, he says it again and again, using way too many exclamation points—how outers and others are dangerous. How the Province needs walls and walls and walls! Not just the wall Vlad already built around the bottom of Rulers Mountain. Or the wall around the village at the top. But walls around the *entire* Timeless Province.

When Best Farriver was their Ruler with Magic—*RM* with no *H* at all—visitors from other lands were warmly welcomed. Now anyone who dares cross into their village to visit a relative or a faraway friend is locked up or shipped home. Certainly no one new is allowed to live there with them. And if you dare to speak badly about Vlad's walls . . . *Poof!* You're turned into a silent centipede or a blob of gum. And maybe even worse . . . people are beginning to look at their neighbors with doubt and mistrust. A shameful feeling of anxious suspicion has seeped into the corners of their beautiful province.

Henry and Button reach the sidewalk, where Apollo Dante and his brother Rocco wait for him, along with their sister, Coco, and baby Otto, who is balanced on Mrs. Dante's hip. And now—well, *finally*—we come to a *good* thing that has changed since we first met Henry. Before last summer, Henry was so lonely, his very soul ached. That loneliness was with him every *tick tock* of the clock. But now he doesn't feel that loneliness *every* moment, because he has something remarkable and astonishing: friends. Honestly, he can hardly believe it. Seeing the Dante family there is like finding a giant pile of Christmas presents under a tree. He has never actually found a giant pile of Christmas presents under a tree, but this is how he imagines you might feel if you did. His heart soars.

"Good morning, Henry," Mrs. Dante says. She smiles at him. She ruffles his hair. This is such a miracle every time it occurs that it's worth saying again, with extra enthusiasm: *She smiles at him! She ruffles his hair!*

"Good morning, Mrs. Dante," Henry says. "Hi, Apollo, and Rocco, and Coco, and Otto."

Rocco and Coco aren't listening, because they are busy being siblings. Rocco pokes Coco and she says *Stop poking me!* And then Coco pokes Rocco and he says *YOU stop poking ME.* Otto only says *Blurghy goo gah*, which surely means something quite intelligent in baby language.

What's weird, though, is that this morning, Apollo only looks down at his handsome new shoes and mumbles, "Mmrning, Hry." It's weird because Apollo is very intelligent, and handsome, and confident. He has everything a child could want. He's not the looking-down-and-mumbling type, not at all.

"Show Henry your new glasses, Apollo," Mrs. Dante says.

"We saw Dr. Frederick Valhalla, optometrist and man-about-town, and now Apollo can see much more clearly, can't you, Apollo?"

"I hay mglsss," Apollo mumbles again.

When Apollo peeks up, Henry gasps, because *wow*. Right on his very own face, Apollo has something astonishing and dazzling—a pair of glasses! Round, magical disks of clarity! Oh man! Henry has wished and *wished* for a pair of those for years. Things are blurry for Henry. Very blurry. People look like hungry bears. Bicycles look like fierce monsters charging at him. Playgrounds look like dangerous battlegrounds. It's hard to know what is what.

"Those are really amazing," Henry says, but Apollo only shakes his head and turns red from embarrassment. This is all very hard for Henry to understand.

"Shall we go, children?" Mrs. Dante says. "You should come along, too, Button, and then you can spend the day with me if you like." She pats the dog's head.

Henry and Button and the Dante family walk down their own street and then another one. They stop at a long road that leads to a big field. A blur races toward Henry, a familiar blur this time—a girl wearing sturdy pirate boots and a leather pirate vest over a billowing white pirate shirt. Like Henry, she doesn't have a backpack. Instead, everything she needs for school is stuffed into the many bulging pockets of her pants. She's got a red pirate kerchief tied around her head, and her brown hair, decorated with pirate beads, flies out behind her as she runs.

She's out of breath when she reaches them. "Holy zucchini, Apollo. Cool glasses," Pirate Girl says.

"Thnk yr," Apollo mumbles, his head still down.

*All* of this is new for Henry. Before the terrifying and wonderful events of last summer, he walked to school by himself. But not anymore. Not since Grandfather Every— the senior-most spell breaker alive—revealed the shocking news that Henry and Apollo and Pirate Girl and their friend Jo are (and let's whisper here, since this must be said with extreme care) *spell breakers.* And definitely not since they saved little Rocco from life as a reptile. Now they barely go anywhere alone. *There's safety in numbers,* the caring grown-ups in their life keep saying, but whether this is true or not is impossible to tell.

The world has become *doubly* dangerous for them: Vlad Luxor has no idea that these very regular-looking children are spell breakers, and if he did . . . It's too shuddery to even imagine. Worse, Needleman, Vlad Luxor's right-hand man, *knows* who they are. He's known ever since he first spotted the four children from four particular family lines having a meeting in the Circle of the Y. He has his own reasons for wanting them gone, pronto: If Vlad Luxor discovers that there are spell breakers running about willy-nilly, his right-hand man will be the first to pay. Needleman *himself* will get turned into something awful—a pesky gnat, an annoying wind chime, an extra-fishy salmon loaf.

*An Extra-Fishy Salmon Loaf*

They escaped Needleman's creepy grip once, at that frightening parade and fair, but now he may be lurking behind any lamppost or tree, waiting to snatch them up. So, whenever possible, the good adults of their lives keep protective watch over the children when they're in their very own yards, or on the streets, and, from today forward, on their way to school. Word gets out quickly when a lizard turns back into a toddler. And so—careful whisper to careful whisper—the kind townspeople make a protective net around the four children, guarding against Needleman and his few trusted spies.

Still. We should not forget: Nets have *holes*.

On this first day of school, the small group continues through town. Now they're about to pass the French bakery.

Just before they do, at the doorway of that most delicious-smelling shop, something surprising happens. Ms. Esmé Silvooplay dashes out. She shoves plump, delicious, still-warm DoublaVay Sayes right into their hands.

"To start the year off right," she says.

"Well, thank you very much!" Mrs. Dante beams.

"My pleasure." Ms. Esmé Silvooplay smiles.

"I want one, I want one! Me too!" Rocco and Coco say, and they get their wish. Button is offered a delectable-to-dogs-only Pup Crust.

And then, *another* surprising thing. When they walk past Big Meats, Sir Loinshank Jr. runs outside. He claps the children on the back, jostling Apollo's new glasses.

"For your great coura—" He stops himself. "Well, *you* know." He thrusts a Pork Zoo Chew into Henry's hands—a lion. Apollo gets a hippo, and Pirate Girl gets a giraffe, and Rocco and Coco trade so that Rocco gets the parrot and Coco gets the lemur. The butcher leans down and gives Button a cat Pork Zoo Chew, which she chomps in one bite. Sir Loinshank Jr. tips his cap to Mrs. Dante, and she pretends to tip a hat back, even though she's not wearing one. He gives a wave to Ms. Esmé Silvooplay across the street, and she waves in return.

Next, they pass Creamy Dreamy Dairy, and Miss Becky emerges to offer them delectable Stretch-a-Mile Cheese Cones. It's hard to hear anything over all that gooeyness and crunching. What a remarkable morning!

When they cross the town square, though, and walk by the enormous billboard of Vlad Luxor with the blue scrolling sign on top, it's impossible not to shiver. Anxiety whooshes through all of them like toilet water after a flush. The huge Vlad wears a black tuxedo and a gold crown on his head, and he smiles down with his yellowing teeth. His vacant pinpoint eyes seem to follow Henry with every step.

"Look," Apollo whispers.

Ugh! Not again! Big Walls Make Us GRATE! the scrolling sign says, over and over.

"Grate," Pirate Girl snickers. Henry stifles a giggle, too, but there's nothing funny about it. Besides, they've all learned an important thing—one can reach the height of evil with a large brain or a small one.

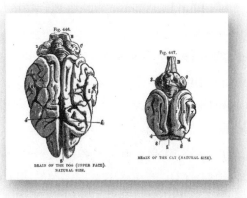

*A Large Brain or a Small One*

"Come on, children," Mrs. Dante says, urging them past that dreadful sign.

Once the scrolling words are behind them, the good cheer

resumes. Rinaldo Francois, from La GreenWee restaurant, crosses the square, his fashionable shoes clip-clipping on the cobblestones. He kisses Mrs. Dante on both cheeks, and bows to the children, accidentally giving baby Otto the perfect chance to grab a fistful of his hair.

"Aie!" he says as Mrs. Dante uncurls Otto's tiny fingers. "May you have a wonderful day, my friends!"

Finally, Jo Idár, her mother, Isabelle, and her two sisters, Luna and Lola, step from the big red doors of Rio Royale, the restaurant Jo's mother owns, and where the Idár family lives upstairs. Henry still finds it a little hard to talk when he first sees Jo's long, shining black hair. She's an exceptionally beautiful and fierce *spell breaker*. His heart flutters like a flower petal in a breeze when he sees her. This morning, under her puffy blue jacket, she wears a T-shirt featuring a warrior on a horse.

"Awesome glasses, Poll," Jo says. "Bye, Mom."

"Goodbye, my pumpkin," Isabelle Idár says to Jo, kissing her cheeks and hugging her. "Goodbye, noodles," she says to Jo's little sister Luna, kissing her next. "Have a great day, sprinkles," she says to Jo's littlest sister, Lola, kissing her, too, and zipping her jacket to her chin. "And this is for you," Jo's mother says to Mrs. Dante, handing her an astonishing cake in pink cellophane. "It's a Cranberry-Craving Élégante Surprise, which is always a *happy* surprise!"

"Oh, Isabelle, thank you!" Mrs. Dante says, and now *they* are kissing and hugging, the two nicest and best mothers

Henry can imagine in the whole world. Next, Jo's mother beams at each of the Dante children, and then gives a special smile and wink to Pirate Girl, who winks back, ever so pleased.

Finally, Isabelle Idár puts her warm hands on either side of Henry's face and looks hard into his eyes with her own brown ones. "Have a perfect first day, little bean," she says, before going back through the two red doors. Henry's heart explodes in fireworks. He gets a nickname, too! He loves Jo's mother so much.

"Look, Jo. Something wonderful," Pirate Girl says, and hands Jo her DoublaVay Saye, her Zoo Chew in the shape of an alligator, and her Stretch-a-Mile.

"Wow," she says. "Yum!"

Right then, Henry realizes *another* thing that's changed for the good, in spite of Vlad's terrible new obsession, and Henry's horrible-as-ever parents, and the lasting feeling that danger is everywhere. As they turn left at the edge of town—just before Huge Meadow, which leads to the Circle of the Y, where one road leads down to the lighthouse and one road leads up to Rulers Mountain, where beyond that is the whole Hollow Valley and the Wilds and the Jagged Mountains—Henry thinks of the ever-so-slight bounce in the steps of the shopkeepers as they greeted the children. Their shining eyes. The quick lift of a smile. It's the same way he feels when he visits his grandfather, Captain Every, or when he sees the beam of the lighthouse.

It's hope. The tiny glow of faith that *maybe* things won't be this dark forever.

The townspeople feel that glow of hope because of *them*, Henry understands. They turned Rocco back into a boy. And, well, shortly afterward, there was also that unfortunate and unsuccessful attempt to turn Mr. Reese, Vlad Luxor's former left-hand man, from a squirrel back into a human as they promised, but never mind that. Hope does not require perfect outcomes in order to glow, which is one of the nicest things about it.

Rocco makes armpit farts all the rest of the way to school. Coco tries to step on the backs of his shoes. Lola and Luna are holding hands and skipping and singing their favorite song at the top of their lungs: *Baby Arugula! Oh, Bay-bee Ah-ru-gu-la!* Apollo keeps his head down, but Jo and Pirate Girl are chatting away about the speed of jaguars versus tigers. When they reach the curve of grass that leads to the steps of their school, Mrs. Dante kisses each of them goodbye. She counts to three, and Lola, Luna, and Coco grab hands and race to where the little kids line up.

"Come along, Button," Mrs. Dante says, but Button refuses to budge. In fact, she sits down beside Henry and fixes Mrs. Dante with her firm gaze. "Well, all right. I suppose no one will mind *this* particular dog at school." She ruffles Button's furry chin before setting off for home with Rocco and Otto.

After all of his first-day jitters, Henry can't wait to go inside. He walked to school with friends, and he received delightful surprises, and Jo's mother gave him a nickname. He has his favorite teacher this year, the kind and thoughtful Ms. Fortune. The fall air smells delicious. The treats have kept him full and warm. His feet shush when they walk through fallen leaves. The tiny feeling of hope—Henry has it, too.

But autumn is a season of change. *Tick, tock.* The clock hands fall forward. The leaves transform into brilliant colors and then drop, turning to a smushy, rotten black. Branches that are so fluffy and orange go bare and spiky. The yellow light turns gray. The pleasant chill in the air turns icy. Fall is a beautiful doorway of illusion, because once you're through it, there's only winter and more winter.

Right then, a big gust of wind rushes through like a terrible ghost in a hurry. Henry looks up. The sky has turned silver and the trees at school are shushing and swaying. A spinning flurry of leaves are carried off. Button's ears fly back, and Pirate Girl puts her hand to her red kerchief so it doesn't blow away. Henry's hope turns to unease, because that's the thing about change—it can happen in a second. Bad to good. Good to bad. In fact, change is coming very soon.

No. It's coming *right now.*

"Oh no!" Jo says in horror. "Oh no. Look!"

## CHAPTER 2

# A Weird and Terrible Spell

Suddenly, Henry can see *two* awful people. First, Jason Scrum, the meanest boy in his school. He's standing right smack in front of them with his hands on his hips. Jason wears his usual camouflage pants and denim jacket, and his haircut is the scariest one of all the possible choices.

*All the Possible Choices*

Jason Scrum is an even meaner bully than Arthur Farley, or even Ginger Norton. Arthur Farley and Ginger Norton are sneerers and taunters and name-callers, same as Jason

Scrum. But Jason has a way of finding the cruelest and most hurtful names. He says the kinds of things that drill far, far down into your heart, things that make you cry and feel small, and even make you wonder if what he says is true. He's made Henry and Pirate Girl feel this way many, many times, and even Jo and Apollo, too. Jason is also the sort of bully that other bullies flock to. They buzz around him like flies on cow manure. And like cow manure, you try to step around him as carefully as possible.

On this morning, though, stepping carefully around Jason Scrum will be totally and completely impossible. He's standing directly in their path, and he's staring straight at Apollo. He's got that look on his face, as if a rocket of nastiness is about to be launched.

You'd think that walking past Jason Scrum would be the worst of the worst, but when Jo said *Oh no!* she meant *OH NO!* It's awful, and you may want to squinch your eyes shut, because there's an even bigger bully than Jason Scrum strolling right down the road in front of their school. The biggest bully. The most evil and frightening person alive.

Vlad Luxor.

Vlad Luxor himself, sauntering as if he doesn't have a care in the world, because he doesn't. When you're the most powerful meanie that exists, the most horrible of horrible mortals alive, *care* is something you can just toss aside, as if it's a snotty Kleenex.

Oh, it's dreadful. The ants flee into sidewalk cracks, and

the wind tries to blow away, and even the ground seems to tremble in an earthquake-like shudder. Thank heavens the little children have already gone inside! Henry shivers in terror. Beside him, Apollo and Jo and Pirate Girl do, too, and Button hovers behind Henry's knees. Henry's so scared he can barely look, but when he peeks, he sees that Vlad Luxor is wearing a velvety purple tracksuit. His stomach splurches over his waistband like a half-filled water balloon, and he has a gold crown in his poof of soft swirly hair. He's carrying a bag from Cadabra. Ah! The poor people in that store!

Now Vlad Luxor reaches into the bag and takes out a garish gold hand mirror. He gazes into it, smoothing his bristly brows and smiling at himself with his yellowed teeth. And then he keeps staring into it as he walks, transfixed by his own image, as if he's gazing at an especially hypnotic picture.

*An Especially Hypnotic Picture*

He stumbles a bit, because it's hard to gaze admiringly at yourself and walk at the same time. Honestly, it's hard to do *anything* very well when you're constantly admiring yourself, let alone wield enormous power. Still, right then, the children are lucky, very lucky, that Vlad Luxor is mostly preoccupied and sees only his own image. If they're all as quiet as they can be, maybe he won't even glance up at the school. All around Henry, the children stop screeching and running around. They freeze in place. The teachers stop blowing whistles. Crows stop cawing, and woodpeckers stop pecking, and worms stop worming.

But one person doesn't stop what he's doing: Jason Scrum. It's like he doesn't even notice Vlad Luxor walking right toward them, which seems impossible. But Jason is so involved in his cruelty that he doesn't see his own end coming, which is a rather common occurrence for bullies throughout history.

"Apollo Dante!" Jason Scrum sneers. "What are you *wearing*?"

They all have bigger worries with Vlad Luxor right there in the distance, of course. Still, Apollo's face crumples, and Pirate Girl's cheeks flame with anger, and Henry's heart aches for Apollo.

"Are those *glasses*?" Jason cackles. "Four-eyes, four-eyes," he sings. "That's what you get for being a bookworm!"

"Ignore him," Jo whispers as softly as she can.

Jason Scrum's face is twisted, because cruelty always makes a person ugly. Across from him, Apollo, full of despair, stands next to Jo and Henry and Pirate Girl and Button, who are all edging closer and closer together because Vlad is getting nearer and nearer with each step. The wind picks up. It blows hard enough to swirl the leaves right at their feet, and it howls through Henry's thin clothing.

Vlad Luxor is almost in front of the school. Pirate Girl's fingers slip into Henry's and grip hard. You can almost *feel* Vlad Luxor right there, like you feel the flu—a puke-y, fever-y wrongness. But Jason Scrum only sees Apollo's glasses.

"How many fingers am I holding up?" he taunts, raising two fingers and waving them around.

Apollo's eyes fill with tears.

"How do you even see out of those things?" Jason Scrum taunts. "Hahaha! You look *so weird.*"

And this is when it happens: Change. Magic. A certain event smushing with another event, causing a fateful shift.

Because at the *exact* moment those words leave Jason Scrum's lips, Vlad Luxor reaches the grass hill in front of the school. Jason's words are loud, *very* loud, since a hush of fear has fallen over the whole schoolyard. *You look so weird* sounds like *YOU LOOK SO WEIRD.*

Henry gasps. It's one of those times when you know exactly what's going to happen before it even does. Henry flinches and squinches his eyes shut just as he hears Vlad Luxor roar.

"WHAT DID YOU SAY TO ME?"

With one eye, Henry peeks at Jason Scrum, and what a sight. Jason Scrum's own eyes have gone wide as dinner plates, and his mouth is open, and he's turned as white as a sheep in a snowstorm. What is more horrible, but also a little bit great, if Henry is being honest, is that Jason Scrum is so terrified that his knees are practically knocking together.

"I— I— I . . . ," Jason Scrum says, which is about the worst thing he could say.

"YOU, YOU, YOU? DO YOU THINK EVERYTHING IS ABOUT *YOU*?"

"I m-meant . . . ," Jason stammers. "What's weird is—" He points his finger, which is now about the worst thing he could *do*, because the finger that's trying to point at Apollo shakes and wavers and trembles in the air, hovering in the general direction of Vlad Luxor himself.

"ARE YOU CALLING ME *WEIRD*?" Vlad Luxor thunders. "I'll show you WEIRD, you hideous little brat."

Jo has turned away so she doesn't have to look, and Apollo covers his face with his hands. Henry shuts his eyes hard again, and lifts his shoulders in protection. Pirate Girl's fingers tighten around his. Beside him, Button whimpers.

"There! That will fix you," Vlad Luxor mutters. Henry hears him tromp off, and when he dares to open his eyes once more, Henry sees that their kind teacher, Ms. Fortune, is in the doorway of the school, with tears streaming down her face. Apollo has gone still as a statue, looking utterly astonished. And where Jason Scrum had just been standing, there is now one of the *weirdest* creatures you've ever seen in your life.

*One of the Weirdest Creatures
You've Ever Seen in Your Life*

## CHAPTER 3

# The Weight of Duty

H oly panini!" Pirate Girl says.

"Wow! What is THAT?" Jo breathes.

"I believe that's a gerenuk, also known as a giraffe gazelle, *Litocranius Walleri*, native to East Africa," Apollo says.

What a shocking sight! "His neck *is* very giraffe-like," Henry says.

Pirate Girl snickers, and in spite of the terrible and scary thing that's just happened, Henry gets the giggles, too. Even normally unfunny words like *giraffe-like* seem quite hilarious. "Pee-yew," Pirate Girl says, and plugs her nose.

Boy oh boy, Pirate Girl is right. Forgive this dreadful request, but right now you should imagine a horrific odor: barnyard plus cauliflower plus the slime layer at the bottom of the garbage can.

"Oh, *that* smell," Apollo says. "That's from the scent glands below his eyes that release a tar-like substance. Gerenuks also have them on their knees and between their hooves."

"Gross," Jo says.

"Children!" Ms. Fortune cries. "Children, come here! Come here at once!"

In his shock, Henry almost forgot about their wonderful teacher, who's gesturing madly, trying to get their attention. This is harder than it sounds, with her left arm in a cast. They all heard how it happened: She broke it climbing a tree while searching for her beloved parrot, who'd gone missing.

Henry, Apollo, Jo, and Pirate Girl rush to her. Button doesn't, though. She's barking and running circles around the now-transformed Jason Scrum, as if he's a particularly tall and long-necked dog who might want to play.

Ms. Fortune leans down and whispers, "Children! Children, I know that you have special, um, *skills*. You *have* to help him!"

"We do?" Pirate Girl says.

"Captain Every told us that we can't help *everyone*," Apollo says oh so quietly. "Only certain people, when we get a specific, definite *knowing* that we must. It's much too dangerous otherwise."

"Each, um, *situation* is very involved, according to Captain Every," Jo whispers. "It could take *days*."

"If we tried to right every wrong, there'd be no time for school and homework and reading for fun, that's what Grandfather said," Henry adds, even though he's never allowed to read for fun at home. Still, putting themselves in peril in order to help Jason Scrum . . . even *wanting* to . . . well, it seems like Ms. Fortune is asking them to do something nearly impossible, let alone unwise.

*Something Nearly Impossible,*
*Let Alone Unwise*

"I like him this way," Pirate Girl agrees.

"He's a *child*," Ms. Fortune whispers. "And you're . . ." She doesn't dare even say it—*spell breakers*.

"He looks fine to me," Apollo says.

"Maybe a little *weird*, but *weird* is his favorite word," Pirate Girl says.

"That's for sure," Apollo says.

"Maybe *all* spells aren't bad," Jo says.

Henry wonders if Jo is right. Jason Scrum *always* calls Henry weird, for being too thin and too quiet, and for dodging speeding balls during recess, and for wearing shabby clothes. It really hurts his feelings. And now look. Jason Scrum's neck is very, very *thin*. Even so, a weighty crush is filling Henry's chest. He's not sure what it is. *Duty*, maybe.

"And I doubt he can call anyone names anymore," Pirate Girl says. "What kind of sounds do gerenuks make, Apollo?"

"Wow, I can see my house from here," Jason Scrum says.

The children look at one another. Pirate Girl rolls her eyes. "Ugh, great," she says. "He speaks."

"Man, who just dropped a stink bomb?" Jason waves one hoof in front of his scent glands. "It wasn't me."

"Please! Children." Ms. Fortune stares hard at them with her warm brown eyes. "He's one of your *classmates*! This is a tragedy! Isn't this"—she whispers again—"your *duty*?"

As soon as she says that word, the very one Henry had just been thinking, that crush in his chest gets stronger and more sure. And poor Ms. Fortune! Her face is wet with tears.

Honestly, Henry can't bear it. So many awful things have happened to her already. Her broken arm, that attack of appendicitis last year. And Henry's heart split right in half every time he saw one of those flyers about the missing Tookie.

*Tookie*

Henry sighs. "We have to help him."

"Why?" Apollo moans. His glasses fog with emotion.

"I have no idea," Henry says. "But it's like Grandfather told us. I just feel a *knowing* about it." The feeling—it's the *have to* that comes when your parents tell you to clean your room or write a thank-you note to the relative who gave you a five-dollar bill inside a birthday card. Well, Grandfather Every is the only one who's given Henry such a thing, but you get the idea. The point is, it's something you have no choice about, and the certainty of that fact sits in your gut like too much cheese. The spell-breaking feeling, though—it also has a vein of dread and fear and a little dollop of excitement and a great bit of *who knows what will happen next.*

Now Pirate Girl sighs. "I have the feeling, too. I just didn't want to say so."

"*This* is the feeling?" Apollo rubs his chest. "I thought I had to burp after that Pork Zoo Chew."

Ms. Fortune clasps her hands together rather awkwardly in relief and joy. "Oh, children! I'm so *glad.* Thank you. Thank you!"

"This is a better snack than my mother usually makes," Jason Scrum says. He's walking around on his hind legs, eating the topmost leaves of a nearby tree.

Button has given up and plopped down on the grass, the way you do when a potential playmate turns out to be much less fun than you'd hoped. She sighs through her nose.

"He doesn't even seem to realize he's a gerenuk yet," Jo says. "Probably because he can't see *anything* about himself very clearly. But, ugh. I have the feeling, too."

"Do we have to do this *now*?" Pirate Girl asks. "It's the first day of school, and I heard we get to learn about Vikings this year."

"And I've been counting the days before we can do a book report. Mine's going to be about Juana Azurduy, South American revolutionary." Jo opens the flaps of her puffy coat to show them the warrior on her T-shirt. "She was a distant relative, and very good with swords, rifles, and cannons."

*Juana Azurduy,*
*South American Revolutionary*

"I'm sure it will be excellent," Ms. Fortune says. "But all of that can wait!"

"Won't this be even *more* dangerous than last time? I mean, just going back home to get our bikes, let alone anything else . . ." The tremor in Apollo's voice brings it all back to Henry: Their last spell-breaking adventure on Vlad Luxor's mountain. The way Needleman captured them and stuck them in the Cage Lurch. Their frightening escape, and the long, dark night in the thick forest. He shudders.

"I could come with you," Ms. Fortune says. "If you need adult protection."

Henry loves Ms. Fortune, but a bunch of images now flash through his mind: Ms. Fortune falling into a creek, or stumbling and breaking her other arm. They all heard about the time, too, when she reached over the counter at the French bakery and caught her sleeve in the frosting conveyor belt. If Ms. Silvooplay hadn't acted so speedily . . . Well, this is not something you even want to think about.

"Thank you, but that's okay," Henry tells her. "You're needed here."

And it's true. Now that Vlad Luxor is gone, the children are shrieking and running around on the playground again, twirling in circles on the monkey bars until they're dizzy, walking up the slide instead going down, tagging each other and saying *You're it*, and then tagging each other right back and saying *No, YOU'RE it*. It's utter mayhem.

"You're right, of course," she says.

Besides that, Henry knows, spell breaking is not the place for hovering teachers or worried parents. If they had any idea what was about to happen, Apollo's father would rush over or his mother would start calling them every five minutes, and Jo's mother would try to follow discreetly behind them in the catering truck from Rio Royale. Worse, though, the Dantes and Isabelle Idár would be in danger, too.

"Well, we know what we have to do," Pirate Girl says. "And we know where we're heading."

Henry nods. There's only one place to go when you need great wisdom and guidance about spell breaking.

"What about him, though?" Jo asks. "He still thinks he's a boy."

Jason Scrum is walking around on his back legs. "I could eat these all day," he says, crunching leaves. "They're even better than Rainbow Target Pops."

Ms. Fortune tries to clap her hands, but with one arm in a cast, this is impossible. "Jason!" she shouts. He looks over at them with the bulbs of his widely spaced eyes. "Field trip! With your classmates."

"Them? They're so short, like a bunch of babies," Jason says. "I'm not going on some preschool field trip."

Henry sighs. It is hard, so hard, to have a duty. What an impossible weight to carry. This is what Henry feels now, anyway, as he and Apollo and Jo and Pirate Girl and Button and the gerenuk walk down the treacherous road back home to retrieve their bikes. A sense of doom drops over Henry's shoulders like a cape. He feels afraid even before they descend into the Wilds, even before the Shadow edges from its hiding place and they are in the grips of evil, and . . .

Well, let's just say this is how Henry feels before the truly awful things that are going to happen actually do.

## CHAPTER 4

# A Tree Saves the Day

This is the most boring field trip ever," Jason Scrum
whines. "Are we there yet?"

It's an annoying but somewhat understandable question,
because they've taken the long way through town—the
back way. *The back way* means winding down alleyways
and passing the hidden parts of any village: overflowing
trash cans and unwelcoming stairwells, stacks of empty
crates and cardboard boxes, and even a few rats zipping
around from hiding place to hiding place, making it hard for
Button to focus. The back way is necessary, though, since
they don't want to be spotted and captured by Needleman,
and being spotted is almost a guarantee when you have a
stinky, long-necked, and very opinionated gerenuk with you.

They retrieve Jo's yellow bike from the back of Rio Royale,
and then fetch Pirate Girl's amazing red bike with the sidecar from the house in the big field where she lives with her
father. Apollo sneaks through the side door of his garage to
get his bike without Mrs. Dante or Rocco or Otto hearing,

which isn't hard because Rocco has the television blasting and he's singing the theme song to *Rocket Galaxy* at the top of his lungs. Now they just need to get Henry's bike without his parents seeing.

"Shh," he tells Jason Scrum. Henry has to hurry. It's rather difficult to hide four children, three bikes, a dog, and a creature who's half giraffe, half gazelle, all waiting nearby, and he can't risk getting caught. Henry's home is dangerous and unpredictable and sad even on an ordinary day, as we've mentioned. In fact, poor Henry is so lonely there that he and Button often feel like the sole survivors of a shipwreck.

Henry edges past the rhododendrons to the side yard with the garbage cans. This is where he keeps his bike, which he bought for two dollars at a neighbor's yard sale. It's one of his most prized possessions, along with his lucky rock, his

*The Sole Survivors of a Shipwreck*

*Ranger Scout Handbook*, and two gifts from his grandfather, *Amazing Stories* magazine and the book *Sinister Forces* by Alvin Westwood, all safely hidden from his parents.

Henry's bike leans against the fence. He can hear the

television inside his own house, too, and a loud clattering of pots and pans. Thank goodness—maybe his parents won't hear anything, either. He folds his fingers around the handlebars as quietly as possible. He's just about to exhale his relief when his mother's voice comes booming out from the very walls of the house.

"What is that noise?" she shouts.

Oh no! Henry wrestles his bike past the rhododendrons. He tries to go as fast as he can, but bike wrestling is never easy. His sleeve catches on a rhododendron branch. A wheel bumps a tin can that missed the trash.

"What noise?" Henry's father shouts back.

"Some strange animal out front, I'm sure of it."

It's not him she hears after all, Henry realizes. It's

*The Extraordinary Ears of a Bat*

Jason Scrum, who has unwisely ambled onto the weedy grass of Henry's front lawn. He's eating the few remaining leaves off the lone tree in their yard, making *mmm, mmm, mmm!* sounds. Henry swears his mother has the extraordinary ears of a bat.

"You're crazy! What would a strange animal be doing out front?"

"You never believe anything

I say!" Mrs. Every shouts. "The least you could do is go check! You don't even care about my safety!"

"Of course I care about my safety!" Mr. Every shouts back.

Henry's heart starts beating hard. They've got to get out of there, fast. In his rush, he knocks a lid off of one of the garbage cans, and it clatters to the ground.

"I HEARD THAT, YOU BEAST!" Mrs. Every yells.

"Hurry, Henry! Hurry!" Apollo quietly urges. Apollo has been inside Henry's house. He knows the dangers there.

The bike is finally out the side gate. Apollo is sweating with nerves. Henry flings one leg over his bike just as the front door of his house shoots open.

And now there's Henry's father, with his mean black hair, and prickly whiskers, and gaping mouth that twists and snarls. Mr. Every's eyes swivel across the scene: the gerenuk, the children, and Henry himself.

"HENRY EVERY!" his father yells. He flies down the rickety porch stairs, shaking his gorilla-sized fist.

"Come on, Henry! Come on!" Pirate Girl pleads, because Henry has indeed frozen. This is what happens whenever his father or mother is coming at him, ready to smack or grab or pinch or shake. As you can imagine, a grown-up towering over you stops you right in your tracks. It utterly halts all your good sense and ability to flee. This occurs right in the moment, but it can last a long while afterward, too.

Mr. Every is down those steps now, his face full of rage,

and Mrs. Every follows behind, waving a broom in the air. She spots Jason Scrum on their lawn and screams, "Shoo! Shoo, you hairy, malodorous monster!"

Mr. Every reaches the lawn. The one, poor tree in Henry's yard has roots that lift from the ground like the veins in an old man's hand, and since both roots and veins are life-giving things, the root catches Mr. Every's toe and sends him sprawling.

Mr. Every yells something that cannot be repeated here. Mrs. Every flies down the stairs with the broom and tumbles right over Mr. Every.

"YOU TRIPPED ME!" she yells from the pile of bodies they make on the grass, and then she begins to sob. It's not the kind of sobbing that makes you feel sad and want to help, though. It's the kind of sobbing that's trying to make you feel bad, and so this is what unfreezes Henry.

"Pedal, Henry! Pedal!" Jo says, and then he does. He pedals and pedals with the speed of fear, and the terror of a fast-beating heart.

## CHAPTER 5

# A Nerve-Racking Ride

All the children are pedaling madly now, and Button is running as fast as she can, and so is Jason Scrum, more gazelle than giraffe at the moment, showing surprising grace and elegance for a bully.

The terrible experience at Henry's house, the narrow miss—it sends them back through the alleys and to the edge of town with shocking speed. At one narrow turn, Pirate Girl's sidecar even causes a pile of boxes to fly midair, sending various fruits and vegetables scattering, same as in those movies with a motorcycle chase in an exotic locale. They can't stop to restack the boxes, though, however much they want to. Speed, however rude or hazardous, is the important thing. Henry even has to swerve rather dangerously around a grapefruit, which is sitting directly in his path.

*Directly in His Path*

When they ride past the billboard to reach the edge of town, the children notice that the sign has already changed: DIFFERENT IS DANGEROUS! WALLS ARE THE WAY! Do you see how shocking things have gotten? New messages are coming practically every minute! There is no time to shiver or cringe, though. They keep going, bumping down onto the dirt path of the meadow. In the summer, that meadow was filled with blue and white and yellow flowers, but now the grasses are orangey and red and golden, more damp than sneezy. Jo is in the lead. She arcs her arm over her head to urge them to keep going, same as Juana Azurduy must have done with the rebel army.

Finally, they reach the Circle of the Y, where one road leads down, down to the Indigo Sea, and another leads up, up the mountain road to the tower. Henry has been pedaling so hard that he's barely looked at the tower until now. He stares upward, and, oh, it's creepy. Fifty-eight stories of black mirror, rising so far into the sky, he can barely see the top. The tower casts a huge, dark shadow, and Henry's stomach begins to ache. It's the gnawing feeling you get in the nearness of evil, like a fat rat chewing on the edge of your favorite paperback.

Henry's eyes dart around, and Button's ears twitch. Needleman could pop out at any moment, with his pointy nose and reaching fingers. He'd love nothing more than to find them here, alone and out in the open.

Jo drops her bike. Pirate Girl hops off, too, and so do

Apollo and Henry. The cuffs of their pants are wet from riding through dewy grass. Pirate Girl passes around two water bottles that she had in her sidecar because she's always prepared. She makes a cup with her hands and lets Button drink from them.

"That was terrible back there at your house, Henry! Are you okay?" Jo asks with her usual kindness.

Henry nods.

"It was just like *Captain Steve Savage: Operation Destruction*," Jason Scrum says. "I wasn't scared, though. Everyone else was scared, but not me."

*Captain Steve Savage:*
*Operation Destruction*

Pirate Girl rolls her eyes. Jason Scrum's gazelle-giraffe eyes had clearly been terrified when Mrs. Every came at him with that broom. He took off like a, well, a *gazelle* being chased by a lion.

"I don't need any water. I'm not the least bit thirsty," he brags.

"Gerenuks can go their whole life without drinking any-thing," Apollo tells them, wiping his misty glasses with the hem of his shirt. "They get all the water they need from plants." Thank goodness Apollo knows such a vast array of facts.

Jason is standing on his back legs again, crunching some leaves on a tree near the Circle of the Y. "*Gere*-what? Are you calling me names? This field trip sucks so far."

"*Gerenuk*. A member of the antelope family, with particu-larly bulgy eyes and big horns."

"Horns?" Jason says with his mouth full, which means it sounds more like *Hrms?*

"Oh, never mind," Apollo says. He shakes his head in exasperation, but Jason has already turned away, his atten-tion only on his own hunger and needs. "How is it possible that he *still* doesn't see what he's become?" Apollo asks the others.

"Well, he couldn't see what a beastly human he was before, so maybe he can't see what a human-ly beast he is now." Jo has a good point.

"All he thinks about is Jason, Jason, Jason," Pirate Girl says.

"What do you want? Are you calling me? Can't you see I'm busy?" the gerenuk gripes.

"I wish we could leave him here," Henry says. "But I think we'd better bring him to Grandfather's, same as we did Rocco."

"Let's hurry," Jo says. They're all thinking the same thing. It's not just Needleman they have to be afraid of. Vlad Luxor's spies are everywhere, too—spies who tattle to Vlad whenever they catch anyone saying something bad about him. Think what a prize it would be to tell Vlad that *spell breakers* exist!

The children look around uneasily. The wind sounds like whispers, and a rustling tree like the flap of Needleman's coat. Henry can still remember the feel of Needleman's chilly, spindly fingers on the back of his neck.

"Yeah, let's get out of here," Jo says. "I'm getting the creeps."

"Don't worry, Jo. At least I have *this*." Pirate Girl rummages around in her pockets, locates her pocketknife, and holds it up in the air. "Ta-da!" she says, catching the attention of the gerenuk.

"You *always* have a stupid pocketknife. It's so *weird*," Jason Scrum says, making a face at Pirate Girl as he walks around on his hind legs.

"Don't listen to him, Pirate Girl," Henry says, which is quite brave, given Jason's nasty past. "Come on, let's go."

It's astonishing how, bit by bit, Henry begins to feel better as they head down toward the sea. His thin legs feel stronger when the sky begins to widen. His spirit feels sturdier when he first smells the ocean. And when he actually sees the red and white stripes of the lighthouse in view, that revolving beam that never dims in any darkness or storm, well, his heart soars. With every swivel of the lantern, the bright light tells Henry (and anyone else who needs it) something quite important—*Blink, there's a safe place in the world. Blink, you won't be lost forever. Blink, you are never as alone as you feel.*

Oh, how Henry loves this place. When they finally reach the lighthouse, and the majestic white house with the red shutters that sits alongside of it, the children drop their bikes and race with Button through the gate of the white fence, past the bank of ivy, and up the steps of the white porch. Jason Scrum is already there, naturally, since gerenuks can run nearly thirty-five miles an hour. He's on his hind legs again, walking around the old tree out front, which has only a handful of fall leaves left on it.

"Where are the trees in this place? All I see is a great big bunch of water! This is the worst field trip ever!"

"Oh, Henry! We're here!" Pirate Girl's eyes dance with happiness.

Henry's heart thuds with excitement. He reaches out to

knock on the door, but right then, the door opens. And it's too joyous for words, because there he is: Henry's grandfather, Captain Every, the most senior spell breaker alive, the wisest and warmest and most wonderful everything you can imagine, standing there in his crisp blue captain's uniform, which stretches over his big barrel of a chest. Henry ducks right into the curve of his arm, and Captain Every gives him a kiss on the top of his head, like a perfect cherry on a sundae.

"What do I see here?" Captain Every booms. His arms are out wide, and they are just the kind of arms you want to run into. Button hops up around the captain's knees. Grandfather looks at each of the children, even Jason Scrum, wandering around the front garden inside the tidy white fence of the lighthouse.

"We have a problem," Apollo says.

"Yes, yes," Captain Every says. "I've noticed. There's a long-necked and terribly stinky gerenuk in my yard. However, I also see a bookish young man with a very admirable new pair of spectacles, and a girl pirate with ready pockets, and another girl with a brave warrior on her shirt, and a thin, kind boy without a coat on a cold fall day, and a devoted little dog who understands how important it is to be a good friend. I must say, this is the most beautiful collection of weirdness any man could ever hope to find on his front porch. Come in, children. This calls for a celebration."

## CHAPTER 6
# A Delicious Reunion

W ait," Pirate Girl asks. "What about him?" She hooks her thumb toward Jason Scrum, who is rubbing his smelly head on a rock. "Does he get to come in, too?"

"Of course not!" Grandfather says, to Henry's great relief. "How could we bear the smell? And I never, ever let a bully into my home."

Jo flings her arms around Captain Every's wide middle. Henry does the same. They all feel the kind of joy you do when a large and powerful grown-up says just the thing you need to hear.

"But what if he wanders off?" Apollo asks. He lowers his voice, even though they are safer at Grandfather's than anywhere else. "I mean, we're here because we all got that strange, strong feeling that we must help him."

"If he wanders off, he wanders off! Bullies aren't the most sensible sort. In fact, most of the time they're great big dum-dums, or they wouldn't be bullies at all. Did I already remark on those handsome new glasses, dear boy? My, they are quite a pair. Did I ever tell you about my good friend Commander Paolo Dupaul? Before he got his specs, his vision was so fuzzy, he saw two of everything. Two anacondas, two battleships, two Uncle Edwards."

*Two Uncle Edwards*

"How annoying!" Jo says.

"Two pyramids, two treasure chests, two drowning sailors! Even if there was only a single entendre in front of him, he saw *double* entendres!"

"What's an entendre?" Apollo asks.

"Treasure chests?" Pirate Girl asks.

"Why, once he even—"

"Big!" Down the short path from the keeper's house, the door of the lighthouse springs open, and The Beautiful Librarian pops out. "You didn't tell me the children were here!"

"I was just about to, my darling, the minute we stepped inside, away from that stinky bully."

"Ugh, yes. I see him or, rather, *smell* him. Quite right," she says. The Beautiful Librarian, well, obviously she's very beautiful, with her elaborate hairdo, sprayed to perfection, and her own pair of serious glasses perched on her nose, and a shimmery dress the shimmery orange color of autumn itself. But better than her beauty is the way she lifts Henry practically right up off his feet in order to hug and kiss him, something he never stops finding incredible, since this never happens to him at home. Another spectacular thing about The Beautiful Librarian is her great intelligence and the very special something she watches over in that lighthouse. Henry catches only a glimpse of it as she slips out the door and closes it behind her. It's a place that never stops being shivery-amazing, the kind of amazing that takes your breath away. A place he can't wait to see again.

You may have noticed another remarkable thing, the same remarkable thing Henry has. "How did you already know, Grandfather, that the gerenuk is actually a bully? I mean, before we even told you?"

"Why, his abnormally long neck, of course, and his bulgy eyes, and his rather lovely, I must admit, eyelashes, and the terrible stench that clouds around him like a fart after a big burrito."

Pirate Girl begins to giggle, and then they all must pause and giggle for a moment, naturally. In spite of the great danger they're in, in spite of the despicable state of their world, one must always stop to laugh. In fact, if they were *not* giggling at something so hilarious, it might be cause for alarm.

Now, though, as they walk farther into Grandfather's house, Henry and the others notice a smell that is most definitely not terrible. It's the very opposite of terrible, a smell that is wonderful and delicious, one that practically lifts you up into a warm hug, same as The Beautiful Librarian's. Maybe one of the best smells in the world— the smell of something baking. Warm butter, sweet browning sugar, every sort of spirit-rising goodness. Henry realizes that the bully's condition is not all that Grandfather somehow knew before it actually happened. He was expecting them, as he always seems to, even before they arrived.

The smell pulls them straight to the dining room, where all of their mouths drop open, even Button's.

"Holy Houdini," Pirate Girl says, and indeed, it seems as if some great magic has just been performed, because an absolute *feast* is spread out on the table. Henry sees plates of scones with jam, and plates of jam with scones. He sees melons artfully arranged, and Clam Hideaways, and a Five- Tier of Beef. He sees a tray of refreshing beverages and a fine cake on a large doily, and even six dishes that cannot be identified.

"Wow," Jo says as Apollo rubs his hands together in glee.

"Well, have a seat and dig in," Grandfather says, "as we discuss the tragic events that have brought us together again."

*Six Dishes That*
*Cannot Be Identified*

## CHAPTER 7

# A Sad Secret

And just like that, *poof!* Jason Scrum became a gerenuk," Pirate Girl explains, with a bit of whipped cream on her cheek. "Though I didn't even know there was such a thing until today."

By the time Pirate Girl reaches the end of the story, The Beautiful Librarian has polished off two scones and a Clam Hideaway, and Jo has had seconds of Dish Four. Button's own bowl has been licked clean. The something on Dish Six, which was buttery and tart and sweet all at once, still melts on Henry's tongue. Oh, it's so wonderful being at his grandfather's house, where his tummy is full and satisfied instead of empty and howling, just like the wind is now.

"That is absolutely awful," The Beautiful Librarian says. "That he is such a meanie, I mean. Please pass the scones." Jo slides them her way, plucking one from the plate first.

Henry sips the last slurp from his straw, licks the slippery saltiness from one finger and the sticky sweetness from another. Apollo jabs his fork right into the remaining bits of the second Tier of Beef. Pirate Girl makes an empty clam-shell clack like a castanet. Finally, The Beautiful Librarian finishes her meal and tosses her napkin to her plate.

"Let's get down to the business at hand, shall we?" she says.

"Ah yes," Grandfather sighs. "Turning the bully back into a boy."

"But why, Captain Every? Why do we have to try to turn him back into a boy?" Apollo asks, pushing his dish away. His glasses are tilted on his nose from all the reaching and grabbing. "We each got the strong feeling that this is one of the spells we *must* break, just as you told us we would, but none of us really *want* to help. It seems like a lot of trouble for a bully."

Henry nods after Apollo speaks. It's the very thing he was thinking. They all look toward Henry's wise grandfather for an answer.

Grandfather wipes his mouth with his napkin. "Ah," he says. There's a long, long silence, where all they hear is the clock *tick tocking* in the living room, and Button snoring beneath the table, and the waves crashing outside. Grandfather clears his throat. "Well . . . ahem. My darling, might you explain?"

"Yes, um," The Beautiful Librarian says. She brushes scone crumbs from her dress. "It *is* difficult to comprehend.

There aren't always immediate answers to why one must do what one must do. Sometimes we only find out later. But adventures *always* bring us to exciting, unexpected places."

81546

El Don Motel
U. S. 101 (Santa Ana Freeway)
Between Santa Ana and Anaheim, Cal.

*Exciting, Unexpected Places*

"Well said, darling."

"I don't understand," Pirate Girl says. She sets her crumpled napkin beside her plate. Her Clam Hideaway castanet gapes silently.

"Precisely!" Captain Every says. "You don't understand until you *do* understand. We must do the *what* before we see the *why*."

"But Jason Scrum is horrible," Pirate Girl goes on. "He's always calling everyone *weird*. He says the way I dress is weird. The way I wear my hair. How I carry a pocketknife everywhere. I *love* my pocketknife. It hurts my feelings."

"Ugh, how hurtful," The Beautiful Librarian agrees. "Yuck."

"He said my glasses were weird," Apollo says. The memory makes Apollo's face squinch with upset. He blinks hard so he doesn't cry. "He always calls me a bookworm. He makes fun of me for having the answers and for reading all the time."

The Beautiful Librarian gasps. "For *reading* all the time? For being *intelligent*? What nonsense."

"He's called me *weird* hundreds of times. Because of my clothes. And because I'm too thin. Because I'm quiet and shy sometimes," Henry says. He's shy *a lot* of times. Most times. Even *remembering* Jason's mean words makes Henry bite the edge of his thumb with sadness. "He teases me whenever we have to play dodgeball."

"Grr. This is making me madder and madder," The Beautiful Librarian says, and Grandfather just shakes his head as if there are too many baffling things rolling around in it.

Jo hasn't said a thing, Henry realizes. And now, when he looks over at her, he sees tears rolling down her cheeks. It's awful.

"Are you okay, Jo?" Pirate Girl asks. She scoots a saucer of jam out of the way to take Jo's hand. Even Button wakes from her nap and emerges from under the table. She stares at Jo with her soulful eyes, because dogs are highly sensitive and especially kindhearted creatures.

"I . . ."

"It's okay, Jo," Henry says, though he doesn't know if this is actually true. There is a lot that is definitely not okay.

"Tell us what's wrong," Pirate Girl says.

"Jason has *always* made fun of me. Mostly for liking math. He says girls aren't good at math."

"Ludicrous! I am a whiz at long division," The Beautiful Librarian says. "Fractions and geometry, too!"

"It gets worse, though. Way worse. Because . . ." Jo puts her head in her hands. Her voice is so low and muffled, Henry has to lean carefully toward her to make out the words. "I didn't even want to tell anyone about this. But he teases me and teases me about my mom and Becky. 'Your mom likes a gir-rrl.' No! My mom *loves* Becky, and I love my mom, and Becky, and our whole family. It makes me feel awful."

Poor Jo can barely speak. Seeing her cry like this, her shoulders going up and down in sorrow . . . a giant swell of sadness rises up in Henry, but so does a big wave of fury. He loves Jo's mom and Miss Becky, too. Isabelle Idár has the nicest brown eyes, with smile crinkles at their corners. When she looks at Henry, when she looks at *all* of them, it's like she's proud, even if they're not doing anything special at all. And Miss Becky . . . anytime Henry has ever walked past Creamy Dreamy Dairy, she's doing something thoughtful—helping Miss Red from the bookstore pick out a cheese, or giving Vic Chihuahua two extra eggs with his dozen. Henry is so upset. He's heartsick, like when you find a magnificent creature washed up on the beach.

*A Magnificent Creature Washed Up on the Beach*

"And now my mom and Becky are having a celebration of love in *two days*. In the farthest corner of Huge Meadow, at the golden hour of twilight. The safest and most hidden place at the most beautiful time there is, and I've barely been able to talk about it," Jo cries.

"A celebration of love?" Apollo asks. "Is that like a wedding?"

"Kind of. My mom doesn't want to get married. But they want to celebrate their love and being a family, and it's hard for me to even be as happy as I should be, because Jason Scrum has been so mean."

Grandfather Every leans forward, his elbows on the table.

"Excuse me, my child, but I think I must have misheard. Did you say that the boy was cruel about *love*?"

Jo nods.

"Despicable," The Beautiful Librarian says.

"Wait. I must be mistaken," Grandfather says. He tilts his head and sticks a finger in one ear as if he has water in it. He rubs his eyes as if they're cloudy. "I thought I heard you say that the boy was cruel about love! And then when I asked you if this was true, I was quite positive you nodded! Which is ridiculous, of course. *No one* would make fun of the greatest, most powerful, most enchanted and important thing we have in the universe, greater even than light and knowledge."

"I *did* say that, though. I *did* nod. Jason Scrum told me it was wrong and weird so many times that he almost made *me* believe it."

"*Cruel* about *love*!" Grandfather says.

Now something extraordinary and fantastic but also somewhat frightening occurs. Grandfather Every slams both palms on the table, making the dishes and glasses tremble. His face turns red. Not a regular red, but the fiery-hot shade of the sun. He pushes his chair back and stands. His chest fills until the buttons of his jacket look like they might pop. He clutches his heart. For a moment, Henry is filled with a terrible worry, because he has never seen his grandfather like this.

"Big?" The Beautiful Librarian says. Her face is concerned, too. "Are you all right? Is it your heart?"

"OF COURSE I AM NOT ALL RIGHT!" he booms. "OF COURSE IT'S MY HEART! THIS IS A TRAVESTY!"

"A travesty indeed," The Beautiful Librarian says.

"Cruel about *love*! Who on earth would be that horrible? No one! That is preposterous! That is outrageous! That is almost beyond belief! Why, cruelty about love—that's a crime against our majestic universe and our natural world! Our very humanity! All the mysteries and splendors of life on earth!"

Grandfather shakes his head again. *"Cruelty about love."*

Henry has so often seen his father's face turn red, and his mother's voice boom, that he immediately feels that same cringing inwardness, that same anxiety, and the curve of his back begins to sink into his chair. Just as it does, though, Grandfather notices him.

"Oh, Henry," he says more softly. "Henry, my boy." He sits back down and takes Henry's hand and gives it a squeeze, and Henry realizes that this is the same grandfather he's always known.

*All the Mysteries and Splendors of Life on Earth*

56

"I'm not angry at any of you here. I'm angry about the dark and nasty side of human nature! We should all be angry about that." It's hard for Henry to take this in—that sometimes, anger is the right thing.

"Jason Scrum has made us *all* feel bad and wrong and weird. Do you see why we don't want to break this particular spell, Captain Every?" Apollo says.

"Yes, yes, indeed I do. And now I see why you have to try."

## CHAPTER 8

# A Place of Marvel and Wonder

Grandfather rises again, and almost before Henry can blink, the great captain and The Beautiful Librarian are hurrying through that wonderful living room with the fireplace and the mermaid statue and the captain's chair with the embossed anchor on the back. The children follow, through the open door, and then to the front garden, where Henry can see the beach and the whitecaps of the waves beyond.

On the path to the lighthouse, Grandfather is walking so fast that it's hard for everyone except Button to keep up. The Beautiful Librarian is rushing along right beside him.

"Have you noticed the timing of this spell, Big?" Henry hears her ask him. "Just as that lunatic is going on about walls, walls, walls."

"With Avar Slaven, it was—"

"A chain-link fence, with barbed wire at the top," The Beautiful Librarian says, her head bent toward his. "I thought we'd never return to that vile time in our history, but the evil is amping up."

"Degree by putrid degree," Grandfather says. "The poor children. Things are getting worse and worse."

"Are there any postcards in this place?" Jason Scrum says, wandering upright around the lawn. "The least I should get is a key chain."

"What will we have to do to break the spell, Captain Every?" Apollo asks, practically running. "Will we be home before dinner?"

"I can't be gone long!" Jo says. "My mother's celebration is on *Saturday*. I can't miss it."

"Are you thinking of Mr. Chester White Pig?" Henry hears The Beautiful Librarian ask Captain Every.

"Yuck! I'd forgotten all about that swine. No. I was thinking of the Reverend Monoxide."

"That awful man who turned invisible? We *were* happy to see him gone, so that seems quite close, but I'm not sure."

"Well, we better think quickly, because this is an emergency. Cruelty like that spreads like mold on a bun."

"Oh, it's always so difficult to unravel the threads of evil, let alone in a hurry. Let me see. Aunty Freeze was cruelty, but more that cold and silent variety, and I do think—wait, Big. We're here."

"When are we having lunch?" Jason whines. "I want salad."

The Beautiful Librarian rolls her eyes. "Ugh! I don't know

how you're going to bear such selfishness," she says to the children, who've finally caught up. "A terrifying new adventure is stressful enough without the headache of bad behavior with you."

The Beautiful Librarian turns the knob of the lighthouse door and they step inside. Henry can still hear Jason Scrum—*A nice, big salad with lots of leaves*—until she shuts the door behind them. For a moment, they huddle in this comfortable small room that has everything a person might need—charming paned windows that look out toward the sea, and a cozy reading chair, and a large bed with down-filled fluffy pillows. On the little stove there's a kettle for warm tea, and in the pantry are tins of butter cookies. It's the most snug and welcoming and cheerful hideaway you can imagine, but the children go quiet. It's the kind of quiet you feel in an important place, a hush of respect, because they know what's beyond that room.

Henry has been here many times before, when he's managed to sneak out and visit his grandfather. Henry and Jo and Pirate Girl and Apollo and Button have all been here together before, too—when they needed to turn Rocco from a naked lizard back into a boy, and when they attempted that unfortunate spell-breaking episode with Mr. Reese.

But this is a place you could go hundreds and hundreds of times and still feel what the children do at that moment: a quiet excitement that starts at your toes, filling you like a balloon that almost lifts you right up off the ground.

Because beyond that little square room is the most incredible and wondrous library you've ever seen—a library that swirls and rises up to the very top of that lighthouse, with books upon books upon glorious books. There are ancient books and new ones, musty sneezy books and crispy shiny ones. Books tiny enough to fit on a teaspoon, books large enough to sit on. Books about leathery crocodiles and the ancient Sahara desert and flashing comets and astonishing gondolas on the Venice canals.

*Astonishing Gondolas on the Venice Canals*

"Can we?" Jo whispers, her eyes wide. Henry knows exactly what she's asking, and he knows exactly what the answer will be.

"*Can* you? Of course! You *must!*" The Beautiful Librarian beams.

So they take off running, because even in times of great

emergency, you must revel in the astonishing beauty and power of books. The children dash up those curving stairs to the very top of the lighthouse library, their fingers running along beautiful spines and their noses sticking into pages to inhale the wonderful smell of them. Pirate Girl finds a volume about sailing ships, and Apollo finds a hardback about unexplored lands, and Henry finds a story about dragon slayers, and Jo finds a biography of Ada Lovelace, mathematician and the first computer programmer ever.

*Ada Lovelace,*
*Mathematician and the First*
*Computer Programmer Ever*

Of course, as you already know, it's easy to get lost in a book, since in those pages you find delicious escape, and the noisiest, most exciting quiet, and fascinating facts. You can totally forget about mean parents and troublesome gerenuks and even great evil, and this is almost what happens. Henry and the others just begin to tumble headlong into the stories on their laps when The Beautiful Librarian—keeper of the knowledge, as Grandfather Every is keeper of the light—calls out.

"Spells!" she commands.

Hard as it is to do, they set down their books and dash back to the large curved table in the middle of the lighthouse. The Beautiful Librarian has a single volume laid out on the table, a small book with a leather cover and gold tipped onto the ends of each page. It's open to a place near the beginning. The Beautiful Librarian taps a paragraph with her finger.

"I think this is the one, Big. Actually, I'm sure of it. Do you recall Mrs. Ivy Sumac?"

"Ugh, poisonous woman. Rather short, lived by the stream. Quite territorial."

"Just thinking of her makes my skin crawl," The Beautiful Librarian says.

"She had that run-in with Avar Slaven. Yes, yes. I think you're right."

"He was the HRM of your time, right, Grandfather?" Henry asks. *Avar Slaven.* The name gives Henry the serious creeps even now, when he's been long gone.

"Indeed he was. And one day, Avar Slaven wandered into the forested area where Mrs. Sumac lived. She thought he was an intruder, there to take what was hers. And then she yelled, 'Get away, you weirdo,' and waved a banana threateningly."

"Not a banana, Big. Something much more dangerous. A flyswatter."

"Oh, that's correct, my dear. Avar Slaven was outraged, and while he was a very, very evil man, I must say, her behavior *was* outrageous, since what she thought was hers really belonged to everyone. Still, right there on the spot, he turned her into a . . . What was it, darling? A chimpanzee? A donkey? My memory is sketchy," Grandfather admits.

"A Sparklemuffin," The Beautiful Librarian says.

Pirate Girl giggles.

"A what?" Jo asks.

"Sparklemuffin," Apollo says. "An Australian spider with a red-and-blue-striped midsection. It does an unusual mating dance where it waves one leg around."

"Making it very, very—"

*"Weird,"* Henry says, interrupting her.

"Exactly," The Beautiful Librarian says, and beams at him.

"Weird like a gerenuk! Was Ivy Sumac cruel about love, too?" Jo asks.

"Oh no. But she was cruel to people who were born somewhere else."

"Cruelty about being born somewhere else?" Henry can't imagine it.

"I know. It's preposterous," Grandfather says.

"That's the silliest thing I've ever heard," Pirate Girl says.

"She was cruel if a person was born somewhere else, and she was even cruel if their *parents* were born somewhere else, or their grandparents, or their great-great-*great*-grandparents."

"Cruelty because your great-great-great-grandparents

were born somewhere else?" It's so ridiculous, Henry would laugh if cruelty were in any way funny, which it never is.

"I know. It makes no sense whatsoever, of course. But people can find the oddest and most outlandish reasons to be cruel. Why, I once knew a boy who made fun of my large nose."

"You don't have a very large nose," Jo says. "Not compared to many others."

"Well, one could take all of the noses off all of our faces to measure, but I hardly

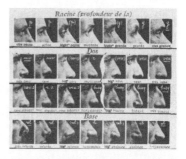

*Many Others*

see the point in that. Every face has a nose if it's lucky, and everyone must be born somewhere, and if everyone were the same, why, we'd never tell each other apart! In fact—"

"Big. Let's stick to the story of Mrs. Ivy Sumac. After Avar Slaven turned her into a Sparklemuffin, you got that feeling, remember? The strong one that insisted you had to help even though Mrs. Sumac was a bully. It seemed like a fine idea, actually, for her to be a spider, since we *should* scream and run from people like that. Still, even though you did not yet understand *why*, you set out to help. This was the spell you used. And let me just say right here that I think your nose is quite handsome."

"Why, thank you, my darling," Grandfather says, pleased,

before perusing the spell. "*Bizarro Crueltildo.* Yes, yes. This is it. Oh, I hate to even tell them about this one."

"I know," The Beautiful Librarian says. "This is awful news."

A terrible clunk of dread settles into Henry's stomach. Jo has turned pale.

"Apollo, my friend. Give those spectacles a whirl and read it for us," Grandfather says. Pirate Girl looks nervously at Henry, who looks even more nervously at Jo. Apollo pushes his glasses up. He stares down at the important curls of cursive. He clears his throat.

"'*Bizarro Crueltildo.* Duration: somewhat permanent,'" Apollo reads. "'Spell-breaking option number one. Accompany victim to a large gathering involving music, particularly stylish attire, and high spirits . . .'"

"Well, that won't work this time, will it, Big? I mean, the children aren't old enough for a disco."

"Definitely not."

"Still. You should tell them the story. Do you remember— the twenty-first night of September?"

"However could I forget?"

"What's a disco?" Pirate Girl asks.

The Beautiful Librarian puts one finger to her lips to shush Pirate Girl in the most gentle way imaginable. "Go on, Big. Tell them what happened to Mrs. Sumac. Or rather, the very important thing that *didn't* happen. Tell them the bad news."

## CHAPTER 9

# The Bad News

"As the spell required," Grandfather begins, "I took Ivy Sumac to a dancing establishment, popular at the time. But before I did that, I changed out of my captain's uniform, and into particularly stylish attire."

"You must have been a sight, Big," The Beautiful Librarian says.

"Powder blue was surprisingly flattering. Once I was dressed, well, if you read forward in this rather lengthy

*Particularly Stylish Attire*

spell, you'll see that the next aim is to seek an unexpected outcome among flickering lights."

"That doesn't sound very dangerous," Apollo says.

"Precisely why I chose option one and not option two, which is utterly terrifying and immensely perilous. *No one* would want to choose option two. So, I shoved Mrs. Sumac right into my pocket and headed to the packed dancing establishment, where the music was as loud as a squalling baby with rhythm."

"Did something unexpected happen to Mrs. Sumac?" Jo asks.

"Indeed it did. What I *expected*—well, to take a Sparkle-muffin to a disco would no doubt bring on a great deal of pointing and laughing and ridicule. I was sure that both Mrs. Sumac and I would leave feeling abundantly humiliated. I set her on the floor, which was rather worrisome in itself, because there were quite a lot of glittery platform shoes, boogying madly around."

"Boogying?" Pirate Girl asks.

"An old-fashioned word for dancing," The Beautiful Librarian explains. "Go on, Big."

"Instead of the embarrassment that I was sure would be coming any minute, something extraordinary happened," Grandfather says. "Mrs. Sumac, with her flashy blue-and-red midsection, did her one-legged mating dance. Suddenly, the crowd erupted into cheers. It *was* actually quite breathtaking, I must admit. The other dancers cleared the floor and gathered around to watch. And when she was finished, instead of jeers and taunts, everyone applauded."

"Wow," Henry says. "Did Mrs. Sumac turn back into a bully right there?"

"This is where the bad news comes in. The spell didn't work."

"It didn't?" Pirate Girl says, looking rather alarmed.

"Why not?" Apollo asks.

"I have no idea!" Grandfather says. "Admittedly, the lights were *flashing*, not exactly *flickering*, which might have been one problem. *Somewhat permanent* might have been another. Honestly, I didn't investigate further."

"Because you moved right on to the terrifying option two?" Jo guesses.

"No, not at all. Because Mrs. Sumac was happier than she'd been in years. The positive attention quite lifted her self-esteem. I'd forgotten something important: Music has its own timeless and ever-present magic. The matter seemed settled. I hardly gave it another thought. Until now. Until I suddenly realized what this means for *you*."

Henry also suddenly realizes what this means. It's very bad news. It's one of those times when you're sure that nothing good can come of this.

"If the spell didn't work, we're, uh, left with terrifying option two?" Henry says.

*One of Those Times When You're Sure That Nothing Good Can Come of This*

"I'm afraid so," Grandfather says, with a grim face. "Give the specs a second spin, Apollo, my boy."

Apollo's voice quavers. "Well, there's all this smudgy part after option one . . ."

"Ah yes. That's where I spilled my alluring cologne before the big night out. Never mind. That spell had a glitch anyway. Move along, right here, to two." Grandfather points to the page.

"'Spell-breaking option two,'" Apollo reads, "'to be attempted only in emergencies. Repeat: only in emergencies where option one is impossible!'" Apollo looks sick.

"Go ahead," The Beautiful Librarian says, giving an encouraging smile.

"'In a far corner of the world, walk the victim of *Bizarro Crueltildo* along the line between good and evil, falling to the side of good.'" Apollo stops.

"Keep reading," Pirate Girl says.

"That's all."

"That's it?" Jo says.

"Of course that's not *it*," Grandfather says.

"But it doesn't say anything else. What are we supposed to actually *do*?" Jo asks Captain Every.

"A plan will present itself, and then you will—"

"Follow it to great success," Apollo says. "That's what you told us with Rocco, but we followed it to great danger first!"

"And what if we're *not* successful?" Jo asks. "I hate to bring this up, but there was the embarrassing failure with Mr. Reese . . ."

"Pfft," Grandfather says, with a wave of his hand. "Irrelevant. A trivial spell. Five minutes, and no adventure involved, why would magic waste its precious talents on *that*? That spell was a shell with no nut, a case without a pillow, a body with no heart! And you certainly wouldn't plumb the depths of disaster and scale the heights of joy and risk your lives for a single squirrel, now, would you? It's not part of *the larger story*," Grandfather says, waving his arm to indicate the rows and rows of books.

"I guess I *didn't* get the important feeling about Mr. Reese," Pirate Girl says. "I just tried because we told him we would."

"Same here," Apollo says.

"But the line between good and evil . . . where is *that*?" Pirate Girl shivers.

"Well, it could be any number of places," The Beautiful Librarian says. "There are dividers everywhere in the province lately."

"And dividers are always dangerous . . . ," Grandfather muses. "So perhaps some location where bad people are lurking behind every possible tree and lamppost."

"Bad people," Henry whispers. "Needleman!" His horrible pointy nose and long, cold fingers flash before Henry's eyes.

"Vlad Luxor!" Pirate Girl says. "Let alone all his spies."

"The exact places we're not supposed to go," Jo says.

"We're in enough danger just walking to school. This is awful."

"And I can't believe we have to do this all for that bully Jason Scrum, even if it *is* for some important reason we don't understand yet," Apollo says.

"A duty is a duty," Grandfather reminds.

"That bully Jason Scrum," Pirate Girl breathes, as if she just now remembered something important.

"Exactly!" Jo rolls her eyes.

"No. I mean, *Jason Scrum*," Pirate Girl says.

All at once, Henry understands what Pirate Girl is saying. He gets that stop-in-your-tracks panic, like when you realize that your little sister has been way too quiet with your box of crayons, or that your naughty puppy has been left alone with your tennis shoes. *"Jason Scrum,"* he says. "We haven't heard him out there at all. And we've been in here for a very long time."

"Oh no . . . ," Jo groans.

Henry stands on his toes to look out the lighthouse window. And when he does, his stomach sinks. All he can see is the great wide ocean and the long stretching beach.

"He's gone," Henry says.

"Gone? He can't be!" Apollo's voice is shrill.

"This is bad," Pirate Girl says.

"I can't see him anywhere," Henry reports.

"Don't panic, children," Grandfather says.

"Wait! The telescope." In a flash, The Beautiful Librarian is holding it to her eye, looking left and then looking right. "Hmm. Three seagulls, four large waves, one clump of slimy kelp, and one rather impressive sand castle."

*One Rather Impressive Sand Castle*

"No gerenuk?"

"No gerenuk."

"Then, children," Grandfather says, "it's time to panic."

## CHAPTER 10

# A Missing Bully

He's nowhere!" Henry says. They drop their bikes in the Circle of the Y after riding all the way back up, up the road from the lighthouse at top speed. Button is panting. Pirate Girl's cheeks are red from the effort of pedaling against the wind. Now they can see practically all the way down the meadow road to town. There's not a single gerenuk in sight.

"If we can't find him, there's no way we can—" Pirate Girl lowers her voice. She doesn't even dare say it—*break the spell*. Now that they're back outside, they have to be careful, since Vlad Luxor's spies seem to be everywhere lately. Just last summer, the spies stayed mostly on Rulers Mountain, but since Vlad has been going on and on about *inners* and *outers* and *others* and *us*, it's like Vlad Luxor has lifted a giant rock, and all sorts of yucky things are wriggling out into the daylight.

"Let's think about this logically," Apollo says quietly. His glasses have fogged from the steam of exertion, and it's

74

almost hard to see his eyes. "Gerenuks spend their days looking for food, and they are very picky eaters."

"Just like Luna," Jo sighs. "She refuses to eat anything yellow."

"Rocco won't eat anything green," Apollo says, and then he and Jo pause to share a look of understanding that makes Henry feel slightly disappointed.

"He's nowhere in this meadow, that's for sure," Pirate Girl says, thankfully breaking up the unpleasant romantic moment.

"Gerenuks don't eat grass," Apollo says, "so no wonder he's not here. They only like broad-leaf plants and trees, and thorny, prickly shrubs."

Henry looks up at the huge mirrored tower, Vlad Luxor's tower. It looms above them, high on Rulers Mountain. He stares at the road going up, up, a road that goes through a—

"Not the forest again," Pirate Girl groans, interrupting his thoughts. They had to spend a horrible and frightening night there when they were trying to turn Apollo's little brother Rocco back into a boy.

"Oh please no." Jo shivers.

"I don't think he's there," Apollo says.

"What a relief," Jo says. Henry lets out a long exhale, too.

"*That* forest doesn't have the kind of wide leaves a gerenuk would like." Apollo bites his thumb with nerves.

"Wait," Pirate Girl says. "What do you mean, *that* forest?"

"You're not saying—" Henry's stomach drops same as

when an asteroid falls from the sky and destroys a planet on *Rocket Galaxy*.

"The *Wilds*?" Jo says. "No. No, no, no. We went to the tower, but *no one* goes to the Wilds."

"All I know about the Wilds is that it's a land of its own. An endless tangle of who-knows-what," Henry says. "You can go in there and never come out."

"My mother said if you ventured into it, you could easily find yourself in places you hadn't intended," Jo says. "That's *way* too dangerous."

"You guys aren't even mentioning the worst part," Pirate Girl says.

Henry can barely think about it, let alone say it out loud. In the Wilds, there's an entirely different kind of enemy. Not a terrifying HRM or an evil right-hand man, but a shocking monster of some kind that few have ever even *seen*.

"The Shadow of the Wilds," Jo breathes. Her face goes white.

"They say it's an evil spirit that climbs trees, walks upright, breathes fire, and kills men," Pirate Girl tells them, as if they needed to hear the gory details right then.

"No way. We can't go in there," Henry says as a trickle of goose bumps shoots up his arms.

"But the Wilds is just the place for a gerenuk," Apollo says. "It *is* a land of its own, with plants and trees of *all* sorts. A grove of ancient baobabs. A whole area of rainbow eucalyptus with bark in every color you can imagine. Dragon's blood trees with thick red sap, and giant sequoias, and even one redwood nearly three hundred feet tall."

"It sounds so amazing that I almost want to go," Pirate Girl says. "Except for . . ." She puts her hands up like a giant scary creature in *Amazing Stories* magazine.

*A Giant Scary Creature in*
*Amazing Stories Magazine*

Apollo shakes his head firmly. "Uh-uh. You definitely don't *want* to go. And not just because of . . . the Shadow of the Wilds." It's hard for Apollo to even speak the words, which is quite understandable if you've heard the rumors. A dragon-like beast hanging in a tree. Twelve feet long. A whip-like tail, a bone-crushing bite. Full-grown men pummeled like piñatas.

"I'm afraid to ask," Jo sighs. "All right. Go ahead and tell us."

"Well, there's a forest of knives, too, made of sharp

limestone rocks that are as high as skyscrapers. It's deadly to even walk by them."

"No way!" Pirate Girl says. "That's horrible *and* extremely interesting."

"How do you know all this, Apollo?" Jo's impressed, and Henry can't blame her, because he is, too.

"I just read about it in *Unexplored Lands* in the lighthouse library."

"He wouldn't go in there, would he? Jason Scrum, I mean," Henry says.

"He only thinks about his own needs, and his need is food," Apollo says. "And for a hungry gerenuk, the Wilds is a menu with practically everything."

Henry groans.

"I hate to even say so, but I'm sure that's where he went." Apollo shakes his head because they're doomed. "In the Wilds, there are definitely broad-leafed shrubs, and even—"

"Shh!" Pirate Girl says. She grabs Apollo's arm to quiet him.

Henry hears something,

*A Menu with Practically Everything*

too. It's some sort of scritching sound, and there's rustling, and even a few grunts and mumbles. Henry's heart bangs like an unlatched shutter in a windstorm. Button begins to growl, long and low. And then, in a moment, there's a flash of movement, the kind of flurry where many things are happening at once. Pirate Girl is flapping her arms. Jo is swatting something away from her head.

And then Jo screams.

G et off of me, you creep!" Jo yells.

Before Henry even understands what's happening, Pirate Girl has Mr. Reese by the collar. Mr. Reese! The former left-hand man, currently a squirrel thanks to Vlad Luxor, is doing the most awful thing you can imagine a squirrel doing—scurrying around in Jo's hair. A few weeks ago, Mr. Reese helped the children escape to safety, but only after they promised to turn him back into a man. Unfortunately, the spell was a failure and had rather surprising side effects.

*Rather Surprising Side Effects*

With one swift move, Pirate Girl grabs Mr. Reese by the wide collar of his cloak. "What do you think you're doing, scaring us like that?"

"And where did you even come from?" Apollo asks.

"That tree right there," Mr. Reese says, straightening his bonnet and pointing his scary little claws toward a large evergreen somewhat far away. "You seem to have given me an ability to jump great distances, even though you've made me an object of ridicule."

"I think you look lovely," Jo says. The corner of her mouth goes up in a smile. "I've seen worse."

*Worse*

Mr. Reese shakes his little fists. "Do you think this is in any way acceptable? What if *you* had to wear this outfit forever? I went through the heat of summer in this coat! Ugh!" He grabs his bonnet with both sets of claws, but it won't lift from his head.

"Pfft," Pirate Girl says, just like Grandfather Every. "Trivial."

"Trivial!" Mr. Reese's cheeks puff with outrage. "How could you say such a thing? If you weren't the only ones around who could fix this embarrassing situation, I would turn around right now and not bother to warn you."

"Warn us?" Henry says.

"He no longer recognizes me in this humiliating outfit, so I ran straight past him to tell you. He's coming your way!" Mr. Reese points down the meadow road. Henry can't see a thing. His own eyes are so bad, all of Huge Meadow is just a blur of orange and yellow.

"Who?" Pirate Girl asks.

"WHO? Who do you think?" Mr. Reese yells as loudly as a squirrel can.

Apollo pushes his glasses up his nose and looks in the direction Mr. Reese is pointing. "Oh no! Needleman! He *is* coming!" A flurry of panic pours from Apollo. "Wearing his dark suit with those shiny cuff links! He's carrying a walking stick, and he's sticking it into every clump of brush, and lifting the leaves and branches, and bending down to look underneath . . ."

Henry shudders. He will never forget Needleman's frigid grip around his neck, or the way he pinched them under their arms, or shoved them into the Cage Lurch, cackling horribly every time the ride spun past him. Just the thought of Needleman's thin, pointed nose jabbing into their faces, fingers reaching . . . Henry is utterly terrified, yet he also has one of those brief moments of courage that take place only in your head.

When the children hear Needleman's cold, awful voice in the distance, though, any thoughts of bravery vanish.

"Children! Oh, children!" he calls. "Little truant children who are skipping school today! Don't you know what this will do to your report cards? You won't get your shiny trophies and first-place ribbons! You won't go to an important college! Your bragging parents will be disgraced by their failed little superstars!"

*One of Those Brief Moments of Courage That Take Place Only in Your Head*

Needleman gets louder and louder as he gets closer and closer. "Oh, chil-dren! Where *are* you?"

"Don't just stand there with your mouths open and your knees knocking! Move!" Mr. Reese says.

"The rodent's right!" Pirate Girl says. "Hurry! We've got to get out of here."

## CHAPTER 12
# Nowhere to Turn

Pirate Girl puts two fingers in her mouth and blows, and at the loud *threep!* Button jumps into her sidecar. Wow. Henry always admires this about Pirate Girl. She knows *every* way to make a whistle with your fingers.

The children hop on their bikes. Henry pedals madly. Jo's

*Every Way to Make a Whistle with Your Fingers*

shiny black hair streams behind her. Pirate Girl leads the way, and Apollo's feet spin in blurred circles.

If it were up to Henry right now, he'd be riding back down, down the road to the lighthouse and to safety. And today, they're not going up, up the mountain road that leads to Vlad Luxor's black-mirrored tower, either. No, they're heading somewhere entirely different, where none of them have ever gone before, and where few villagers have even gone, because, of course, no one with an ounce of good sense would even consider sticking one foot into the Wilds. Past the Circle of the Y, everything that's familiar in Huge Meadow disappears behind them: the orange-tipped grasses of fall, the slumped heads of the dying flowers. The path dwindles to an end, and now there's only the uneven flat land of Hollow Valley.

Henry rides so fast, his knobby tennis-ball knees throb. His small hands grip the handlebars, and the fall chill whips right through his thin T-shirt. Pirate Girl is hunched down, riding hard, too, with Button in her sidecar, but the path is getting rockier and bumpier, and the sidecar jangles and threatens to spill.

"I'm going to get off," Apollo shouts over his shoulder. It's the only possible thing to do, so they all begin to walk their bikes over the stones and through the clumps of grass of Hollow Valley.

Now imagine this: Ahead of you is an immense and

looming wall of green, growing larger and larger as you get closer and closer. It's a huge expanse of tangled brush and bizarre-looking plants that isn't so much a jungle as an entirely new land. The smell is old and wet and green and earthy, and that smell seems to get larger, too, as you walk closer. Once you enter a place like that, your own home, your province, would—poof—disappear, as if you were swallowed by a leafy green darkness.

"Wow," Pirate Girl says.

That place stretches before them like a mystery, like their own unknown futures. Their toes are right at the edge. Apollo drops his bike. Henry sees strangler figs winding their way up every tree, and brain-like witches' butter clumped along roots and branches. He hears strange calls of unknown birds—both *eek, eek, eek* and *awk, awk, awk,* and *eek, awk, eek* and *awk, eek, awk,* and . . . One could go on forever listing them. It's easy to believe there are creatures of all kinds and sizes in there. It's easy to believe there's an evil spirit that can break your bones like a mad teacher snaps a number 2 pencil.

"The Wilds." Henry's voice is full of hushed fear, but he's also awestruck, and full of curiosity, too, because none of them has been this close to it before.

"We'll *never* get out of there before my mom's celebration," Jo says. "We may not get out of there *ever.*"

"There's no way we can bring our bikes," Pirate Girl says.

"It almost looks too thick to even *walk* in," Henry says, putting down his kickstand and scooping Button from Pirate Girl's sidecar.

"This is a terrible plan. I mean, look at that place," Jo says.

"But Needleman will be here any second," Pirate Girl says. "We'll be trapped up against this jungle of . . . *everything*."

"Going in there is a *very* bad idea," Apollo says with great certainty, and the children's faces grow worried, and now you should imagine a feeling of great despair mixed with anxiety, because if you can't go forward and you can't go back, you're in deep trouble.

"It's dark and creepy. But it's also prickly and viny and shrubby and perfect for a gerenuk. Ugh!" Pirate Girl rubs her temples.

"We have to think of another way to find him," Jo says. "And fast."

But they've been standing there far too long already, trembling and pondering. Evil has its own cunning speed, even if it's wearing shiny black dress shoes, and Needleman is visible in the distance now, waving that stick over his head.

"I see you, you little brats!" he shouts. "I see you right there! Caught, with nowhere to turn!"

And he's right. They *are* caught, with the Wilds on one side and Needleman on the other. He's getting so close so fast that Henry can see the drops of perspiration trickling down Needleman's forehead, because, of course, one works up quite a sweat running that distance in a black suit with cuff links. Henry sees the look in Needleman's eyes, too, and he can almost feel his cold grip again, as if Needleman is a creature made only of sharp, chilled fingers.

*A Creature Made Only of*
*Sharp, Chilled Fingers*

Needleman is panting hard. He's right there, so near now that when he waves the stick, Henry feels a whoosh of air. And when he waves it again, the end of it ticks Henry's shirt.

*"Chee chee chee!"* Mr. Reese says, twitching his tail in urgency and speaking squirrel since Needleman still doesn't know he can talk, let alone that he's Vlad's former left-hand man, helping them secretly.

"Brats!" Needleman puffs. "Sniveling, whining, traitorous, br—" He swings the stick again, and it narrowly misses Apollo.

What an impossible decision! Should they stay or should they go now? If they stay, there will be trouble. And if they go . . . Well, who knows? There's only one way to escape Needleman, though. One terrible place he'll never enter. The same place a gerenuk might be.

"Come on! Into the Wilds!" Jo commands, like Juana Azurduy, commander of the rebel army.

And so the children do the unthinkable. They turn toward that deep, deep tangle and flee into that unknown land, with its endless fathoms of green and its dangerous shadows.

## CHAPTER 13

# Into the Wilds

I sn't that marvelous!" Needleman shouts. "You silly brats, doing my dirty work all by yourselves! I'll just sit here and read a magazine while you disappear. Be sure to look both ways! Put on your sunscreen! See you never!" He cackles.

Quickly—very and most unnervingly quickly—Needleman's voice fades behind them, and any path that they had cleared as they ran in closes behind them, too, like the mouth of a predator.

"I can't believe we're in the *Wilds* . . . ," Jo groans with dread.

"I can't believe we're in the Wilds!" Pirate Girl shouts with excitement. She's whisking her pocket-

THE SIDEWINDER, OR HORNED RATTLESNAKE

*The Mouth of a Predator*

knife this way and that, easing their passage through the thickness. Button is up ahead, scooting around and under brambles and bushes quite adeptly.

Henry's nose fills with every lush, fragrant, mush-roomy damp-earth smell. He hears drips and drops and the scurrying of many-legged creatures. Do you know that kind of deep and disappearing feeling you get when you're reading a marvelous book, the feeling where you can barely hear the sounds of the world around you? Of course, every book *is* a wilderness, but that's the feeling Henry is having, only in real life. There's magic and terror and wonder every direction he looks. In spite of his fear and the danger they're in, he says, "Wow. This is beautiful for a terrible place."

"That's for sure," Pirate Girl says. "And now that we're here, we might as well search for a gerenuk. He's around somewhere."

"So is . . ." Jo doesn't say it—*the Shadow of the Wilds*. But they all glance upward into the trees right then, and Henry rubs his arms from the chill of nerves.

"We have to be very careful," Apollo says. "Don't just grab any old branch for balance, or touch an interesting plant, or smell a beautiful flower. Things are not what they seem here. Be on your toes."

"We will," Henry says. He and Button are already experts at that.

"For example," Apollo continues, "it's okay to eat that awful-looking elephant foot yam." He points to a small, round, horribly ugly plant that looks like a purple cabbage gone wrong. "They're actually really good for you. But we shouldn't go near that devil's helmet over there." Now he points to a very beautiful purple flower.

"It's the exact opposite of what you'd think," Jo says.

"This is the weirdest place I've ever seen." Pirate Girl's eyes are wide.

Henry can hardly take everything in. There's a shocking array of colors and shapes, spike-like teeth and velvety petals, spines and spindles, and silvery nettles. There are living things over his head and at his feet, to his left and to his right, at his elbows and up to his chin and—well, you get the idea. There's flora and fauna flourishing far and near.

"What's *that*?" Henry asks. He feels very lucky to have someone along who reads as much as Apollo does. Henry points to one of the strangest things he has ever seen—a group of plants with enormous flowers, each shaped like a fancy jug. Some of the odd blooms are green and some are a deep red, and some of the lips fold softly under, but some appear to have long sharp fangs.

"They're kind of scary," Pirate Girl says. "And that one has water in it. We could almost *drink* from it."

"I wouldn't do that if I were you," Apollo warns. "Those are Nepenthes pitchers. They'll eat anything that gets close enough. It'll swallow a rat whole."

"Eyuw." Jo shivers.

"And there's another reason why you wouldn't want to drink from it," Apollo says. "See how you could sit right on it? Um . . ." He takes a big breath, the way you do when you must say something you'd rather not. "It's a plant that some animals use as a toilet."

*A Plant That Some*
*Animals Use as a Toilet*

Pirate Girl snickers. "That's seriously important to know. Thanks, Apollo. I'm glad I didn't take a sip! It would have been our first bungle in the jungle."

Now, behind them, there's a noise. It's not a scurrying scorpion or a flower gulping a rat whole, though. It's an annoyed and unhappy squirrel who appears to be at his wits' end.

"Why, why, why would you come to a place like this?" Mr. Reese mutters as he scoots and zigzags toward them, lifting his skirts as he goes. "How will you ever figure out how to turn me back into a man if you keep making horrid decisions like this? Do you know how close you were back there to being—" With one of his creepy squirrel hands, he makes that slicing motion against his neck that means . . . Well, you understand, even without the unpleasant specifics. "I can't believe you foolish children are my best hope for becoming a man again. Ugh! I'd be better off trying to beg Vlad Luxor for forgiveness."

"Are you still here?" Pirate Girl says.

"Well, I'm *finally* here. Do you know how hard it is to run in heels? Why do you wear these things?"

"*I* have no idea. Don't ask me!" Pirate Girl rolls her eyes at Jo, and Jo rolls them back. "I like shoes you can explore the world in."

*Shoes You Can Explore the World In*

"Wait," Jo says. "Wait just a minute."

"*Now* what?" Mr. Reese moans.

"Do you guys smell what I smell?" Jo asks.

Henry sniffs, and oh, it is awful. It's terribly unfair and quite horrible to suggest it once, let alone twice, but please imagine an even more horrific odor than the one you imagined before. A stink that still shoves its way through your nostrils even when you've pinched them closed, one that worms its way into your tummy and flops it right over as if you're about to be carsick. Except, in the wide open of the Wilds, there is no rolling down the window for fresh air, because this *is* fresh air. Button is the only one who's happy about this smell. She sticks her nose right up and sniff-sniff-sniffs, because, to a dog, when it comes to smells, the more stomach-turning, the better.

"Holy vomitini." Pirate Girl makes a horrified face.

"We've found him!" Henry says. "Jason must be right around here somewhere."

"Jason!" Pirate Girl shouts.

"Jason!" Jo shouts, too. "We're here!"

"Are you *nuts*?" the squirrel asks. "Lower your voices! How can I keep you children safe, when you insist on doing the most dangerous things! Like announcing your whereabouts to the *Shadow of the Wilds*! Like going farther and farther into this place, heading right in the direction where Vla—"

"Wait a sec," Apollo interrupts. "It might not be Jason. Look." He points toward a very, *very* odd-looking plant.

Picture a single, enormous lily, large enough for a giant's garden. "A corpse flower. Wow, those are actually quite rare."

"Corpse? Eek," Pirate Girl says.

"It's huge," Henry says. And it looks even huger next to small, thin Henry.

"They can get up to two hundred pounds. And, oh!" Apollo says as they walk deeper and deeper into the Wilds. "Look there! Angel's trumpets! I've read about those, too." He points toward a lovely, drooping flower. "They're very dangerous. If you eat them, they can hypnotize you so that you do horrible stuff and don't even care."

"This is all very fascinating and everything," Jo says, freeing her sleeve from a jagged branch. "But I'm getting the creeps. I feel like something is hovering nearby, or maybe some*one* . . ."

Henry has that creepy feeling, too. Like he's being watched, or worse. The creepy feeling slithers like a slim snake shushing along the ground, one that lifts slowly over your shoes, and then twists around your ankl—

"AAAH," Henry screams. Something actually *is* slinking around the thin bone of his ankle! When he looks down in horror, yanking his foot back, he's relieved to see that it's not the claws of the Shadow or even a snake, but a vine, a thick and hungry vine, gliding across his skin and doing its best to tighten its grip around him.

"Don't worry, Henry!" Pirate Girl says. In an instant, she

frees him with one careful whack of her pocketknife. "We'll definitely have to avoid *those*."

"It's hard to know which direction to go," Apollo says. "And it's already after lunchtime, and we haven't even found Jason Scrum, let alone turned him back into a bully."

"Jason Scrum?" Mr. Reese asks. "That horrid little boy?"

"Vlad Luxor turned the bully into a gerenuk," Apollo explains.

"Wait. Wait, wait, wait! You're here in the *Wilds* to risk your lives for a *bully*?" Mr. Reese's tiny squirrel face twists in outrage. "Or rather, risking *my* chance to be turned back into a man if something happens to you while you're out and about? I can't believe you're even here, walking right toward Vla—"

"Shh!" Pirate Girl says. "I hear something."

Henry stops to listen. Yes. He hears it, too, though it's hard to say where it's coming from.

"Get me offa this thing!" Jason Scrum whines. "No one told me there'd be a boat on this field trip! I hate boats. This stupid boat is making me dizzy."

"We found him," Henry says.

## CHAPTER 14

# What the Children Learn by the Pond

I want more treats!" Jason says. "I see them over there, and there, and there! And instead of being *there*, I'm *here* on this stupid boat!"

"It's him all right," Apollo sighs.

"All we have to do is follow the complaining," Pirate Girl says. But now that they've stopped with their ears perked, the petulant bully has gone silent.

It's very difficult to make their way through the Wilds, and listening for the gerenuk is harder than it sounds, because there are other noises, lots of them. There are the slurps and squashes and slips of plants growing and the earth shifting. There are the screeches and squawks of birds and animals. Henry is getting very tired and cold, and he still can't shake the eerie feeling that shadows, *the* Shadow is everywhere. He spots something moving out of the corner of his eye, something thick and fast. He snatches up Button, and Pirate Girl grabs his arm.

"Did you see that?" she asks.

"I think so," Henry whispers.

"What?" Jo asks. "What did you guys see?" Her voice trembles.

"I knew this was a bad idea," Apollo says.

"It was . . . large. Very large. A tail, maybe?" Pirate Girl's eyes scan the area. "But nothing has a tail *that* big."

"Let's get out of here," Jo says.

Walking is difficult in the tangle of everything fantastic and strange, things that look beautiful but are terrible, things that look weird but are marvelous. Another pulsing vine twists rapidly around Henry's ankle, and he has to stop and free himself. Jo points out a flower that looks like a bumblebee, and then one that looks like a duck in flight, and another that looks like a pair of giant red lips. Pirate Girl shrieks when she sees a branch with a row of tiny skulls, but Apollo explains that it's just the seedpods of an ordinary snapdragon. They see an orchid with the face of a monkey, and then an actual monkey drinking from one of the pitcher plants.

"Gross," Pirate Girl says, and Henry has to agree.

Henry's head aches from all the colors and shapes around him, and from all the new facts and possible dangers everywhere he looks. What he feels now—well, imagine those times when you are very excited but a little nervous to play a new, wonderful game, but the instructions go on and on and on. They're never going to find that gerenuk. Poor

*A Very Tiring Exercise*

Apollo looks exhausted, too, as if he's just finished a very tiring exercise.

Mr. Reese is getting cranky as well, or rather, more cranky than usual, mumbling and squeaking like an old bedspring as he tries to keep up. "I don't know why you all insist on walking straight toward—"

"Shh!" Apollo says. "I hear him."

"Thank goodness," Jo says.

"How many times have I told you that I hate water? Water is boring! I have no need to see all this water, water, water!"

"I think the bully is stuck!" Pirate Girl says. "Water . . . It must be a pond or a lake or a swamp, or . . . Well, here it could be anything."

"But a boat? I can't imagine it." Jo shakes her head. "I think he's over there."

"No," Pirate Girl says. "Over this way."

"I'm sure he's straight ahead," Apollo says.

They stand in a circle, scowling at one another.

"We have to go *some* direction," Henry pleads. Quarreling is certainly understandable right then, but it isn't helping. In fact, quarreling has led them to a dead stop, as disagreements often do.

"Juana Azurduy wouldn't take directions, she'd *give*

directions. This way," Jo commands, and marches forward. This isn't like Jo at all, but the circumstances are rather stressful. The hours are ticking past, and this place would be deadly in the dark.

"This is the longest, dumbest field trip ever." Jason Scrum's voice is suddenly quite clear. "Shouldn't we be wearing life jackets? My mother will be very angry that I'm on a boat and not wearing one."

"You found him, Jo!" Pirate Girl beams.

"Wow," Henry says, because the gerenuk is stuck on something that is definitely *not* a boat. In front of them is an enormous green pond with lily pads that are big enough to stand on.

*Lily Pads That Are Big Enough to Stand On*

"Those are incredible!" Pirate Girl says.

They are. The lily pads cover the entire pond, huge circle sitting next to huge circle, each with a delicate raised edge, like enormous yet elegant green plates spread across a tabletop.

"I've never read about *these* before." Apollo's eyes are large behind his glasses.

"It's about time!" Jason Scrum whines. "Where did *you guys* get to go while I was stuck on this dumb boat? Get me off of here."

"You're not stuck at all!" Jo says, and Henry sees that she's right. "Just step back onto the bank. You can get off quite easily."

"I would, if this stupid boat didn't keep rocking! I would in a second."

Henry understands the problem. With every step the gerenuk tries to take, the lily pad buckles and sloshes. Jason looks quite frightened.

Pirate Girl notices, too. "He's scared," she says.

"I'm not scared! I just hate water. Water is stupid. It's much too wet! I can't swim. This is the worst boat ever."

Mr. Reese lifts his skirts, steps onto one of the large dishes of green, and lies down on his back. "I quite like it. It's wavy and rather soothing."

Pirate Girl has already retrieved her rope. "Well, we have to get him off of there if we want to walk him along a line between good and evil, wherever that is."

Mr. Reese pops his little bonnet-clad head up. "Did you say 'a line between good and evil'?"

"Yes," Henry says. "To break the spell, we need to walk him along a line between good and evil, falling on the side of good."

"You don't mean *the wall*, do you?" Mr. Reese says.

"The wall?" Henry asks.

"The wall, the wall, the wall! Vlad Luxor's wall! The one he's trying to build around the whole province! The Wilds, the Jaggeds, and even Beyond the Mountain! Haven't you read the scrolling sign on the billboard?"

"The wall!" Pirate Girl says. "Of course! That *must* be the line between good and evil."

"You can't go there! Vlad himself *and* Needleman have been over there nearly every day. I know, because I've been keeping track of Needleman's whereabouts. We don't want him surprising you out of nowhere! You children need to be kept—"

"Safe," Pirate Girl says. "Wow! You're like our own little rodent spy!"

"You've been watching out for us, Mr. Reese," Jo says. "Thank you! I think you actually *care* about us. Well, we care about you, too." She picks him right up and plants a kiss on the furry marble of his cheek. This is a shivery thing to imagine doing to a squirrel, but nonetheless, Henry's heart also fills for their little protector.

"Care, shmare! Put me down!" Mr. Reese shakes off the

kiss. But Henry can see that he's actually touched by Jo's affection. He shakes his head, and his eyes get a little watery, and he has to clear his throat before speaking. "The point *is*, they've both been at the construction site every day. There've been problems. This obstacle, that crisis!"

"Problems that even hideous magic can't solve?" Henry asks.

"I can't understand it myself," Mr. Reese says. "Things are going wrong every which way, as if it's some sort of impossibility! But if there's a line between good and evil, that must be it. It's right over . . . Well, I don't know exactly. East, near Rulers Mountain. The wall is supposed to start there. I've gotten quite turned around. Somewhere near, I'm sure. If you'd have stopped your yammering on about scientific facts and this flower and that plant, you would have heard me warning you a thousand times that you are likely walking *straight toward it*."

"Oh no!" Apollo says.

"But *oh yes*, too," Jo says. "At least we know where we're going. We can hurry and get home before dark."

"Not *oh yes*! Not at all! Not for a minute!" Mr. Reese is hopping about with anxiety. "That's one of the most dangerous places in the world right now, with that maniac stomping around, talking about *others* and *its*, *inners* and *outers*, keeping 'dangerous people' away when he is the most dangerous person one could imagine! You can't go there! You will surely get turned into a buffalo or a lamppost or, or . . . who knows what! Mr. Apple was nearly baked into a pie! Do you want to become some other dessert that might be devoured in two seconds?"

*Some Other Dessert That Might*
*Be Devoured in Two Seconds*

"It'll be okay, Mr. Reese. As Captain Every always tell us, 'A plan will present itself, and then you will follow it to great success,'" Pirate Girl says, looking at Henry.

He's not so sure about the great success part. Not at all. Not with the way Mr. Reese, in his permanent dress and bonnet, is looking at them now, with his bulgy rodent eyes all alarmed and his creepy squirrel fingers nervously clawing around in the air. The doom in Henry's stomach rises, the way water fills a pool, or a bathtub, or a sink, or . . . well, it doesn't matter, choose any one you'd like. The point is, it's hard not to think of water and more water when you are standing at the edge of an enormous pond, and a gerenuk is making waves, and your tennis shoes are getting soppy.

"Let's get the bully off the boat," Pirate Girl says.

CHAPTER 15

# Something Funny, Something Not

O h, there's a lot of whining and complaining, cajoling and convincing. Apollo holds out a few large, enticing leaves, the kind that Jason Scrum was trying to reach when he stepped onto that lily pad in the first place. Pirate Girl hops up on it, too, and gives Jason Scrum the rope, which he holds between his gerenuk hooves. The children yank and pull and urge him on from the bank.

"You can do it!" Jo says.

"Come on!" Henry encourages.

"Ow!" the gerenuk squeals, because, right then, Button gives Jason a nip on the behind, which propels the bully forward, right off the giant lily pad and onto land once again.

"Great job," Jo says, but Jason Scrum doesn't say thank you. He's lost his manners, or never found them in the first place. Now he lifts his lips and reaches for those leaves like a horse with a carrot.

*A Horse with a Carrot*

"Which way did you say that wall was, Mr. Reese?" Pirate Girl asks. She's already winding her rope back into a neat circle and scouting in the distance for where to head next.

"You must not have heard me clearly. You cannot go to *the wall*. Or, rather, the place where the wall is somewhat built. That is highly, highly dangerous! Think it through, I beg you! Vlad Luxor, going on and on about *others* and *its* . . . Because, if all of you aren't *other*, and he isn't an *it*"—here, he points to Jason Scrum—"well, then I don't know who is."

"I wish we didn't have to," Apollo sighs.

"Same here," Jo says. "It's getting late, and I'm very worried we won't make it home. Tonight, Becky is coming over, and we're all baking the cake for the celebration of love. And what if we have to stay longer? My mother will cancel everything if I'm not there."

"You won't miss it, Jo," Henry says. "I promise. At least, *I hope* I promise. Which direction do you *think* it is, Mr. Reese?"

Mr. Reese zips his lips shut.

"Don't worry," Pirate Girl says. "I've got this." She holds up her wrist and points to her magnificent Tellzall 9-in-1 Timepiece of Adventure, with a glow-in-the-dark compass, weather forecaster, signalling device, and the world's smallest ballpoint pen. "If the wall is near Rulers Mountain, we go east as far as we can. Follow me."

The soft chirps and trickles of the pond disappear behind them, and now Henry mostly hears the squeak and squish of his wet tennis shoes as he treks behind Pirate Girl, up and around thick roots, veiny palm fronds, and strange trunks that wind and spiral to the sky. He sees a variety of frogs, a smattering of spiders, and plants with more prickles than you could count.

*More Prickles Than You Could Count*

"Hey, look at this!" the gerenuk cries. "A fancy, fancy cup. I'm not even thirsty, not a single bit, but how can you resist a sip from a hanging cup that looks fancy enough for a king?"

"No, Jason!" Apollo shouts. "That's actually a plant that some animals use for a toil—"

"Too late," Pirate Girl says as Jason drinks.

"Even better than Juicee Squeezees!" he says.

Pirate Girl snorts with laughter, and Apollo starts to giggle. And then Jo starts to snicker and sputter with hilarity, and Henry laughs and laughs until he's bent over and his stomach hurts. Button catches their mood, and jumps up on their knees. Even Mr. Reese is chortling, his eyes squinched, his small shoulders going up and down.

"Maybe the Wilds aren't so bad after all," Henry says when he can speak again. "Just, the bullies in the Wilds."

"A new flavor of Juicee Squeezee!" Pirate Girl says. "Lime, orange, monkey pee—" This sends them all into hysterics again. Apollo hoots, and Jo grabs Pirate Girl's arm to make her stop, because she can't take any more, and Henry's eyes are watering from laughing so hard.

But then, all at once, just like that, Button jets into Henry's arms with shock and alarm. Mr. Reese shrieks and crawls up Jo's pant leg and into her jacket to hide. Their laughter stops in a second, because a darkness is slowly creeping over them. A shadow. *The* Shadow. With each step it takes toward them, the enormous creature covers the sun bit by bit.

The children freeze. Henry can't even tell what he's looking at, only that it's terrifying, like nothing he's ever seen before. An enemy, for sure. The Shadow must be two hundred pounds and twelve feet long, at least. Part dinosaur, part lizard, with an enormous tail and a square crocodile head. Its eyes are yellow, and they have a straight, staring gaze that slices right through Henry.

"Urgl," Apollo says, the sound of utter terror.

Pirate Girl has her pocketknife out, but truly, against that creature, that knife looks as dangerous as a paper clip.

The Shadow thrashes its tail, crashing it against the ground, and the earth trembles. Its crocodile-lizard-dinosaur feet claw forward, ripping through plants as that tail flattens everything in its path.

Henry's heart has stopped, for sure. His voice is caught in his throat. It's like one of those nightmares where you try to scream but can't. The gerenuk, though—a horrible, pitiful, high-pitched screech escapes his throat. The Shadow's eyes are directly on Jason Scrum.

"Run!" Jo cries.

## CHAPTER 16

# The Sky Darkens

It might be the absolutely worst thing to do, but the children and the gerenuk turn and flee. As he bolts, still carrying Button, Henry madly tries to remember page 110 of his *Ranger Scout Handbook*, sixth edition, *What to do when you encounter a bear*, but the only thing that comes to him is page 184, *Standard Knots*.

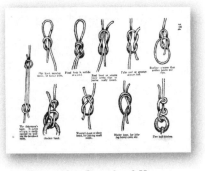

Page 184, Standard Knots

But then *all* thoughts are gone, and there is only the heart-pumping speed of escape. Imagine one of those times you've tried to run faster than you've ever run before, the sort of running that gives you a burn in your chest and a sloshy ache in your guts and twinges in your knees. At least, Henry feels those twinges, and something else, too—stone-cold terror. He's sure he hears the breath

112

of the beast behind him. They run and run and run, until they've somehow crossed out of the jungly area and into a grove of the ancient baobabs Apollo told them about, where the ground is mostly bare except for bright orange dust and dry green grasses.

Jo dares to look over her shoulder. She stops. "It's gone," she says, panting.

"Ow, ow." Pirate Girl holds her side. "I've never run so fast."

"Did you see its eyes?" Apollo says. Apologies for the disturbing details here, but his face has that pale queasiness a person gets before they barf.

"That bully was coming straight at me!" Jason shrieks.

"*Chee*," Mr. Reese says. He's so terrified, he's gone 100 percent squirrel inside Jo's coat.

"It wasn't an evil spirit at all!" Henry says. "It was very, very *real*."

"Who knows when it might pop out again!" Pirate Girl says. "Oh man! I can't believe we still have to go to the wall, let alone back home."

"Home," Jo says with longing. "I wish I was there! That was beyond awful, and now it's getting dark. My mother will be so worried."

"My parents, too." Apollo blinks like he might cry.

"We should keep walking," Henry says. "Until we find a safe place to rest."

"I'm worried the Shadow is . . . *everywhere*," Jo says, putting it perfectly.

"Let's get out of here," Pirate Girl says.

As the children continue east, Jo spots a baboon, and Pirate Girl swears she sees a warthog. Everyone is quite jumpy. Button barks at a lemur with buggy eyes and a striped tail. In the now-dimming light, Apollo warns that they might see the bats who gather in colonies inside the trees. The baobabs themselves have thick round trunks with scruffs of branches only at the very top, like the oldest broom in the house.

They hurry past those huge creased trunks with their dark hollows and, before long, emerge from the baobab forest into a valley of green hills.

"It's so pretty," Jo says. And in spite of the great fright they just had, it is. There are waves of soft, grassy knolls, the sort of hills you'd love to run up and then down, and there's the pleasant sound of trickling water. But Henry's nerves crackle. It's getting late, and cold, too. It's not dark yet, but it's getting there. He doesn't know if the Shadow will suddenly appear

*The Oldest Broom in the House*

here, too, or if it'll stay in the thick green of the jungle, like a crocodile-lizard-dinosaur creature might. The air has that smell of rain coming, and the sky is filling with a gray sea of thick clouds. Henry rubs his arms.

"Wait a sec . . . What was that?" Jason Scrum, gerenuk, says, tilting his globe eyes toward the scowling sky.

"What was what?" Apollo asks.

"I felt something." Jason reaches out with one hoof. "There. I felt it again! This is the worst, most horrible field trip in the world! I almost got eaten! And now *more water*."

A big, fat drop of rain splats right on Henry's forehead. "Oh *no*," he says.

"We're already cold. I am, anyway. We can't get wet, too." Apollo eyes the sky anxiously. "Without shelter, we could die out in the elements, like lots of polar explorers throughout history."

*Plink.* Henry feels another drop on his hand, and then, *plonk*, another one on his ear.

"Very glad for this lovely hat," Mr. Reese says, adjusting its brim.

*Plink, plonk, plonk, plink,* the rain patters, turning from a sprinkle to a shower. Drops fall from the tips of Henry's lashes and ride down the slide of his nose. Overhead, the gray clouds begin to turn as black as the wings of crows.

"What if there's thunder and lightning?" Apollo says. "We're right here out in the open." His glasses have spattered with drops.

"You could use some windshield wipers, Poll," Jo says.

Apollo frowns. He wipes his glasses and puts them on again. "Wow," he says, with the relief of clear vision. "Just a minute! Do you guys see what I see?"

"*No trees* is what I see, and I'm hungry for dinner," the gerenuk says.

Henry squinches his eyes. "I . . I'm not sure," he says. "I see something that looks like a large, scary dragon, slinking across the land."

"It's not a dragon, Henry. It's something good! A river, but not *just* a river," Apollo says. "Hurry!"

Apollo charges down that hill, which is quickly turning a deep, gloomy green, what with the clouds and the night rushing in. The children and Button and the gerenuk and the squirrel all race at top speed behind him, until the dog and the gerenuk overtake Apollo, reaching the spot where he's headed, because it's suddenly quite clear where to go. There's the river, yes, but more important is what's at the very mouth of that river, something tucked like a secret deep underneath those hills.

"It's a limestone cave," Apollo says, breathless.

"Are you sure it's safe to go in there?" Jo asks, peering inside. "It's very, very dark."

Even though the rain is pummeling hard on their heads, and even though the Shadow of the Wilds is somewhere out there, Henry has the same worry. The cave is a mysterious hollow of who-knows-what. All he can see is the river flowing into that arc of black, and the flat bank of rock on either side, both of which disappear.

"This is utter nonsense!" Mr. Reese says, hopping nervously back and forth. "A cave is one big trap!"

"Don't be ridiculous. This is a perfect hiding spot from the Shadow or anyone else, and shelter from the rain, too," Pirate Girl says. "Besides, it's the sort of cave in every adventure story."

*The Sort of Cave in Every Adventure Story*

She steps in, and Button follows. In a moment, the cave seems to gulp them right up. All Henry can see are circles of light from Pirate Girl's flashlight shining this way and that.

"Wow! It's awesome in here!" she shouts. Her words bounce back to them. *Ow, ow, ow. Erè, ere, ere.*

Now even the circles of light vanish, and Henry feels a jolt of terror. Panic flutters in his chest like a hundred bats in a baobab. "Pirate Girl!" he calls. "Button! Come back!"

They're gone, he's sure of it. But maybe not entirely gone, not yet, because a sound tears through that tunnel like a freight train: Pirate Girl, screaming.

CHAPTER 17

# A Sparkling Discovery

S he's screaming, but they're screams of joy and excitement, for once.

"Holy fettuccini! Guys, guys! Get over here, fast!"

*Ast, ast, ast,* the echo commands. But it's dark and hard
to see, and they have to step quite carefully along the rock
bank, since the river is rushing along right beside them.
Jason Scrum keeps stopping, too, whimpering with fear,
and they have to wait patiently for him. When they finally
reach Pirate Girl, where she stands on the large flat bank of
rock, looking up . . . well, Henry gasps.

He has never seen anything quite so magical in all his life,
except for the lighthouse library. This is a magic that comes
from nature, though, not humans. And while humans can
create some extraordinary things, they are *nothing* next to
what nature thinks up.

"Wow," Jo breathes. Button is staring upward, too, with a
sparkle of wonder in her eyes. The gerenuk has gone silent,
and even Mr. Reese can only blink and blink at the sight.

Henry has no words, only awe. Above them, on the huge cavernous ceiling, are hundreds of blue glowing lights, like a sky of cobalt stars. No, like a separate *universe* of cobalt stars, hidden here and glowing for years and years, pinpricks of enchanting, radiant blue, turning the water of the river blue, too.

"*Arachnacampa Luminosa*," Apollo breathes.

"What?" Pirate Girl asks.

"Glowworms."

Volume 10, G.–GOT.

"Wait. I think I read about these in the encyclopedia," Jo says. "Volume Ten, *G.* through *GOT.*"

"It's so beautiful," Henry whispers.

"I've never seen anything like it." Pirate Girl's eyes are wide. "I wish I had a boat that I could float down this river. With all these reflections, it's like a sea of stars."

As they walk farther into the cave, the blue glowing lights are everywhere. They arc in a magnificent sprinkle over the children's heads, and they trickle down the walls to the very edge of the water.

"It's *supposed* to look like a night sky," Apollo says. "So that insects fly upward, right into those threads." He points to the magical strands of glowing blue, shimmering downward like hundreds of tiny meteor showers.

"You might not have a boat, Pirate Girl, but look! That big, flat rock over there looks like an island," Henry says.

"That's where *I'm* sleeping." Pirate Girl is already hopping from one bit of rock to the next to get there. "This is nothing like the night sky we slept under on Rulers Mountain. It's a night sky deep under the earth."

Henry and Button are right behind her. Soon, all of them—even a gerenuk and a squirrel—are perched on the platform of rock that appears to float on that blue river. Apollo and Jo set their jackets on the ground. Pirate Girl removes her leather vest. It's quite warm and snug in the cave. Apollo scoots over so Henry has a place to rest, too.

"You're not thinking of actually *sleeping* are you?" Mr. Reese says. "What is wrong with you people? You need to be alert here in the elements, with a Shadow right outside! And with Vlad and Needleman . . . well, *somewhere* nearby! This is preposterous! You need to keep your eyes open! You need to keep watch! What might happen if you doze off, unaware?"

"Oh, Mr. Reese. You're caring about us again," Jo says.

"I'm not . . . Well, I . . . Ugh!" he sputters.

"We're not thinking of sleeping just yet, anyway," Jo says. "First we have to eat."

"Eat?" Henry says. His stomach is rumbling like belly thunder.

"I guess we might as well make the best of the situation," Apollo says. "And we're as hidden as we possibly can be.

How about lunch for dinner? It's a good thing my parents always pack plenty." He takes his brown bag from his backpack.

"Do I smell Nougat Nut Nuggets?" Mr. Reese's tail twitches. "I'm quite certain I detect the odor of almonds. All right, fine. We'll discuss the watch schedule later."

"Squirrels do have a highly developed sense of smell," Apollo says. "But all I can detect is him." He points to the stinky gerenuk.

"No one said this was a camping field trip," Jason Scrum whines. "I wanna go home! I wanna go home NOW! I'm missing my favorite TV show."

"This is way more amazing than *Rocket Galaxy*," Pirate Girl says, gazing at the hundreds and hundreds of blue lights around them. "We're in a different sort of galaxy ourselves."

"Okay, let's see." Jo removes a cloth napkin from her bag and spreads it out as if they are having a fine dining experience at her mother's restaurant, Rio Royale. "I have two Swiss Goo and Franks, several slices of Pork Pyramid, and a Pineapple Pinwheel we can all share. Also, two packets of Juicee Squeezees, in case you guys are thirsty. Oh, and this." She hands a Nougat Nut Nugget to Mr. Reese as if it's a special gift.

"I knew it," he says, and beams, before ripping the wrapper with his tiny, poky rodent teeth.

"I've got several Juicee Squeezees, too. Also, Yummers

With Cheese and Yummers Without Cheese, a tub of Bologna Bolognese, and a package of eight Crisp Orange Octagons," Apollo says, laying the items alongside Jo's. "And a single Cocoa Nibbler we can divide between us."

"Wow," Henry says. All of these treats are so astonishing that it's hard for him to do what he does next. He hands over his single boiled potato, which has grown as cold and hard as a stone. It looks the way his heart feels—small and ashamed. "I'm sorry. This is all I have."

Next, Pirate Girl removes a small package wrapped in cellophane from her pocket. She unrolls the plastic and offers what's inside: two sad clumps of broccoli.

*Two Sad Clumps of Broccoli*

"I'm sorry, too," she says. The more time Henry spends with Pirate Girl, the more he discovers that they're alike in surprising ways.

"Don't be sorry, you guys," Jo says. "Look! There's plenty for everyone, and the Shadow will never find us in this cave, and we're eating under the stars. Here." She hands Henry and Pirate Girl the Swiss Goo and Franks, and, boy, do they smell amazing. Henry takes a bite. The Swiss is quite gooey, and the franks are plump, and it astonishes him all over again that she and Apollo have things like this every regular day.

"Where's *my* dinner? What do I get? I'll tell you what I want, what I really, *really* want—leaves! Lots of green and crunchy shrubs! Where are they? This is horrible," Jason Scrum whines.

"You've been eating *all day long*," Pirate Girl says.

"So? And how am I ever going to sleep in this place? There are things scurrying around my ankles." All at once, he lets out another very strange gerenuk shriek, and here you must picture the sound of a fork that has accidentally slipped into the garbage disposal. "What was that?" the gerenuk cries.

"Was it white and crawly? Very scary-looking? It might be an albino ant," Apollo says. "These caves are known for those. Maybe it was a giant cricket. There's usually no doubt about those, though. They're as big as your hand."

"Yikes!" Jo says.

"Cool!" Pirate Girl says.

"I'm afraid of insects!" Jason Scrum whines. "And it's too dark in here. Way too dark."

Henry agrees, to be honest. It's dark and hollow-sounding in the cave, and now that he knows there are large insects that might trek over his skin or through his hair . . . Well, he gets that shivery-creepy feeling you have no doubt experienced yourself. But then Pirate Girl speaks.

"There are night-lights *all around* you."

It's a good reminder that light is everywhere, even if it doesn't seem so. It makes Henry remember his grandfather, too, and his house with the always-swiveling beam.

"I need my OWN night-light!" Jason Scrum whines, and stomps his hooves. "I only sleep with my special glittery night-light!"

*His Special Glittery Night-light*

"Ugh!" Apollo says. "None of us are going to get any rest with him around."

For once, though, Apollo is wrong. As you know, large amounts of cheese plus adventure plus a trying and frightening day will cause immense exhaustion, and so, in spite of albino ants and giant crickets and the Shadow, and all the creaky, alarming, *what-might-that-be?* sounds of darkness, Button curls up at Henry's feet. And since a sleeping dog always brings an extra sense of calm and rest, Jo's eyes begin to droop, and Apollo curls up on his side of the jacket and begins to nod off, and Mr. Reese rests on the Nougat Nut Nuggets wrapper like it's a lovely, yet somewhat noisy sleeping bag, and even Jason Scrum finally shuts up and lies down, resting his stinky unlikable self for the night.

But Pirate Girl is still awake. She sits upright with her arms looped around her knees. And Henry is awake, too, sitting beside her. It reminds Henry of their other spell-breaking adventure, after the fair on Rulers Mountain. Now, though, Pirate Girl stares up at the sky that isn't a sky, to the stars that aren't stars but are magical just the same. When Henry looks up there, it's only the magic he thinks of, not the darkness.

"*Everything* in nature is weird, Henry. I never realized it before," she whispers.

"I noticed that, too," he whispers back. "All of those plants and trees and flowers . . . the baboons and the bats and the baobabs . . . the glowworms! Weird and wonderful."

They both stare at the galaxy of blue glowworm stars. "Beautiful, beautiful weird," Pirate Girl says.

"Even the toilet plant," Henry says, and then, oh dear, it starts. They both crack up, but quietly, so as not to wake the others.

"But it really *was* beautiful," she says, and even though

it's not that funny, they start giggling again, because at that hour, and when you're that tired, everything is downright hilarious. Well, maybe not *everything*.

"Should we take turns staying on guard? Two hours on, two hours off?" Pirate Girl asks, which makes them both immediately quite serious again. "I'm scared of the Shadow. And Needleman, too. I know he'd never go in the Wilds himself, but he always seems to know where we are. And we're so close to Vlad Luxor and that awful wall he's building."

"Yeah. We better stay alert since we're out here all alone," Henry says. "I'll go first."

"Thanks, Henry."

Pirate Girl curls up and closes her eyes. After a while, she finally falls asleep in the blue light. The ancient dark cave curves around Henry, and the night noises jangle his nerves. He stays up way past his two hours, because Henry's used to being up at night, listening carefully for the footsteps of his angry father, or the change in the air that might mean a sharp smack from his mother's hand. But even more than that, he decides not to wake Pirate Girl because she looks so peaceful right then. When he remembers those two sad clumps of broccoli, he thinks that Pirate Girl may need to rest as much as he does.

## CHAPTER 18

# The Worst Forest of All

In the morning, Henry wakes up before the others. He props on his elbows and looks around. The cave smells like clay and rotting plums and smooshy stuff, but Henry likes the smell. Button rouses and trots over and licks Henry's face. It's still dark, dark except for the curve of morning light Henry can now see at the other end of the cave. But it's not too dark to notice something very worrying.

One of them is missing.

"Where is he?" Henry says in a panic.

"Where is who?" Apollo's voice is groggy. He stretches his arms and yawns. "Ow, sleeping on a limestone bed is very uncomfortable."

Jo sits up, her eyes blinking. "Oh, we're still here! I was hoping it had all been a dream!"

"It's still dark," Jason Scrum complains. His gerenuk face is all dirty from sleeping on the cave floor, and his fur is sticking up on his head. "And my alarm hasn't even gone off yet. My mother only comes to wake me up after my alarm goes off lots and lots of times."

Pirate Girl's head pops up. "Wait. Mr. Reese." She notices instantly. "He isn't here."

A bad feeling glugs around inside Henry like those times when you drink too much water and can actually feel waves in your stomach. At first, the bad feeling is about shadows and warthogs and creatures who eat other creatures, especially small squirrels. But then it turns to something worse. All at once, Henry can hear Mr. Reese's voice in his head. *I can't believe you foolish children are my best hope for becoming a man again. Ugh! I'd be better off trying to beg Vlad Luxor for forgiveness.*

"This isn't good," Henry says. "What if Mr. Reese lost patience with us? We haven't turned him back into a man yet! What if . . ." It's almost too horrible and urgent to say. "What if he went to Vlad Luxor?"

"He wouldn't do that, would he?" Jo says. "Maybe he's just out looking for breakfast. Oh, I hope he hurries back. We've got to get on with this day so I can get home before my mother's celebration tomorrow!"

"Can we trust a once-bad man turned into a squirrel in a dress?" Pirate Girl asks, reading Henry's mind. "Especially when he's gone missing? He could be telling Vlad Luxor all about us right now! *Who* we are, and *where* we are. We need to get out of here."

"I hate to think he'd do that. He seems to really care about us," Jo says.

"Maybe we better be on the safe side. Mr. Reese *was* Vlad Luxor's left-hand man." Apollo picks up his glasses and hooks them over each ear, and then he puts on his jacket. "We can eat the Luscious Lime Pockets that I saved for breakfast on the way."

"Man, I just hope we get this done fast. Tonight, we're supposed to start gathering flowers for the celebration," Jo says as she ties her shoes.

Pirate Girl shoves her flashlight into her pants, adjusts her pirate scarf, and tugs on her boots. "We'll make it, Jo. Come on. My compass says we need to go out that way, if we're heading east to where they're trying to build the wall." She points to the dark, gaping mouth of the cave. "If there *is* an out."

Button takes a quick but noisy drink from the river and begins to run ahead, droplets flying from her little chin like rain from a speeding windshield. Henry and the other children follow as quickly as possible over the bumps and crags, dips and divots of the cave floor. And thankfully, there is an exit to the cave, one that grows wider and brighter with daylight the nearer they get. But it's hard to feel hopeful when a Shadow might be anywhere, and a squirrel might be a traitor, and each step takes you closer to great evil.

"What if Vlad Luxor is there at the wall?" Jo shivers. "Or that horrible Needleman."

"It's hard to imagine building an actual wall around our entire province," Apollo says. "This place is so huge and sprawling, it would be like putting a fence between two different *countries*."

"It makes no sense at all," Pirate Girl agrees.

"I'm trying to tell myself that if Juana Azurduy could fight twenty-three battles for freedom, we can walk the line between good and evil to turn Jason Scrum back into a boy," Jo says.

"What?" the stinky gerenuk in question says. He tries to stand in the cave, but he's too tall, and bonks his head. "Ow. I can't hear back here. I don't know why I always have to be in the back during this stupid field trip. And what do you mean, turn Jason Scrum back into a—"

Right then, Jason Scrum shrieks so loud, and the noise echoes so loud back again, that Henry feels like he's the amazing Zazel, just shot from a cannon.

The gerenuk holds his two hairy arms with hooves for hands out in front of him.

*The Amazing Zazel, Just Shot from a Cannon*

"What is this? What is going on here? Wait a sec. Maybe I read about this in that book my mom gave me, *Welcome to Puberty*. No, it can't be! I'm still too young for that! And what are *these*?" He waves his hooves around. "Are these *hooves*? And why do I have this strange craving for vegetables when I hate vegetables? Oh no!" The gerenuk's face is suddenly full of horror.

"Jason—" Jo begins gently.

"Something happened while I was sleeping! Some terrible spell for no reason at all, or maybe a bite from one of those awful ants!"

"This happened to you *yesterday*!" Apollo is losing his patience. "Let's just hurry up and get outside again, and then we'll explain everything."

"I know! It was *you*! You weirdos did something to me! Where's the rest of the class? Where's Ms. Fortune? What have you creeps done?"

"You have mud on your face," Jo says. "You big disgrace! Someone should put you in your place, you horrid boy."

"I'd be happy to," Pirate Girl says, glaring fiercely at the bully.

"I vote to leave him with the albino ants," Apollo says.

But instead of leaving the bully behind, the children do another difficult and brave thing. They shake off the yucky feeling of being wrongly accused and continue winding and weaving and hopping from rock to rock toward the bright curve of an exit. Finally, that dark, magical cave is almost behind them, and the morning light is *right there. Morning light*, well, those are two of the most hopeful words that exist, so imagine the shock and horror and betrayal the children feel when they step out into it, and *this* is what they see.

It's a land of gray rock, a land that stretches not only for miles out in front of them, but upward toward the sky, too. This is not just a tangle of exotic plants and trees, grasping vines, and monster insects. It's a treacherous scene of your worst imagining—deadly towering pillars, and tall, jagged spires, and thin, rising needles. An endless labyrinth of pinnacles and peaks and summits of gray rock and more gray rock, all with edges and spikes sharp enough to slice you like a blade through a banana.

Henry gasps in horror. Button cowers near Henry's legs.

"What is *this*?" Jo breathes.

"A forest of stone. A *limestone* forest." Pirate Girl's voice is a whisper.

Well, breathing and whispering, the details hardly matter, because right then, Pirate Girl reaches out and . . . "Ow! These are razor sharp!" She hurries her bleeding finger to her mouth.

*"The Forest of Knives,"* Apollo says.

This is what it looks like to Henry, too. Knife upon knife upon knife.

*Knife upon Knife upon Knife*

132

"You told us about it, Apollo, but I never imagined *this*," Henry says.

"It's much more awful than I thought, too," Apollo says.

"Hooves! WAAAHHH!" Jason Scrum cries. For the hundredth time, he can only see himself. "What has happened to me?"

"Shush!" Pirate Girl says. "Can't you see we have enough to deal with right here? Mr. Reese might be a traitor, and who knows where the Shadow is, and Needleman or Vlad Luxor might find us at any second, and look at this scary place! Besides, we already told you, you've been a gerenuk for a full twenty-four hours already."

"A gerenuk? I thought those things had horns," Jason Scrum says. He puts one hoof to his head. "NOOOO!"

"Even walking *near* these pillars could be dangerous!" Apollo's eyes are huge behind his glasses, and the Luscious Lime Pocket he'd begun to eat has left a circle of green around his mouth.

"Wait. Aren't gerenuks stinky?" Jason Scrum asks. "Because I smell like a beautiful flower. Every one of *you* smells like the back end of a cow, though."

"How will we ever get through here? Let alone to the wall and back before my mother's celebration." Jo's voice wobbles, and her eyes fill with tears. Oh, Henry's heart is about to break when he sees her like that.

"Are you sure there's no other way through the Wilds, Pirate Girl?" Henry asks. This route looks impossible.

"I'm sure. I guess we'd better wind our way through there." She points to her right, to the maze of tall, thin spires stretching east. "The only other way is over that thing." Now she points to her left, to a large and towering spiky summit, which sits between them and their destination like a giant guard at a gate. The river that rushed through the cave seems to flow around that summit or through it or under it, it's hard to tell which. It's not as high or as massive as the peaks of the Jagged Mountains, of course, but climbing *that* giant would be the last thing Henry would want to do.

"Even if we come to a dead end in this place, we can't even *think* about scaling that. No way. Absolutely not," Apollo continues. "If you were up there and fell and landed on one of those knife trees . . . You might get *impaled*."

"Impaled?" Pirate Girl asks. "What's that?"

Apollo shivers. "You don't even want to know."

*You Don't Even Want to Know*

"We'll get through the maze as quickly and carefully as we can, then, so we can get back before the celebration,"

Henry says. *Quickly* and *carefully*—he might as well have said *impossibly* and *absurdly*.

"And we'll stay as low to the ground as possible. We won't climb up, no matter what." Apollo pats Jo's shoulder, which just adds to Henry's despair.

Pirate Girl has her bandana in her teeth, and all at once, there is a loud *riiip*, and then another and another. She offers the strips to her friends. "Wrap these around your hands for protection," she says. Pirate Girl thinks of everything. "Button, you stay very close to Henry."

Imagine a time you had to walk through a crowded space that was so jammed that you could only go single file. In spots, the children have to turn sideways to fit, and every so often, after squeezing themselves right and then left through narrow passageways, there's a glorious opening up of space where they see the sky and can breathe again. Apollo, with his backpack, gets wedged in one stone corridor, and the children have to yank on his arms to free him. Thin Henry manages to navigate more easily than anyone else, and so he takes the lead. The children wind and weave around stone pillars until it's hard to tell if they are actually going forward or around in circles, because gray rock looks pretty much like gray rock everywhere they look. The fall day has the muggy, smothering feel of clouds about to rain, and Henry wipes his forehead with the bandana tied helpfully around his palm. Henry sees a lizard tail scoot through a crack in the stone. A snake slips past him and then vanishes. He hears the screech of a hawk, and a bird cackling, and a ring-tailed lemur saying *hmm, hmm,* as if he's perplexed. Henry spots a monkey with unusual facial hair, and points it out to Apollo.

"A bearded emperor tamarin," Apollo says. "Our swim instructor, the sarcastic Mr. Cutting, has a mustache like that."

*The Sarcastic Mr. Cutting*

But then the children hear another noise, the kind of noise that stops you in your tracks, especially in such a danger-ous foreign landscape. It's the slurping-smacking sound your little brother makes when he sucks up one noodle at a time, only this is much, much worse. And then there's a *crunch, crunch, crunch,* rather like your annoying sister eat-ing ice. But be assured, this is no brother or sister. This is a terrible sound.

A chilling sound.

A *predator and prey* sound.

Suddenly, Henry gasps. Up ahead, lying across their path—it's the Shadow. Apollo grabs a pinch of Henry's T-shirt to stop him from going forward, but he would never, not in a million years, be able to go forward. Henry's not even sure he can breathe. His lungs feel just the way they did that time when he fell off the monkey bars and landed flat on his back.

"Ah, ah . . . ," Henry says.

The Shadow of the Wilds is stretched out in gluttonous glory. And it's eating something that looks like Beef Glop Rondelee with Tomato Puree, but is definitely not Beef Glop Rondelee with Tomato Puree. Its tail is so long, it disappears up and around a column of stone until you can't see the end of it. Its teeth glint. It licks its rubbery lips. Button leaps into Henry's arms.

There is no possible way around it, which is how all of life's most difficult situations feel at first. But this is no time for wisdom and deep thoughts. The Shadow swivels its head at a sound they haven't even made yet. Its yellow eyes, with their black diamond pupils, lock on Jason Scrum. They have to get out of there, and fast. And in that moment, every single one of them knows there's only one terrible thing they can do.

CHAPTER 19

# Of Course They Go Up,
# You Knew They Would

When you're fleeing a terrible crocodile-lizard-dinosaur-Shadow-something, you move with extraordinary speed. You climb higher and faster than you've ever been before without stopping to think about it, even if *up* is the worst possible direction. Henry's tennis shoes skitter on that gray rock, jamming into toeholds, as he pulls himself higher using each jutting stone. He's thankful for Pirate Girl's bandana, bound around his hands, or his skin would surely get as sliced as Ham Streamers with Gravy.

"Don't look down, Henry," Pirate Girl says. "We're so, so high!"

He's trying not to. It's somewhat difficult, because the Shadow has ambled over to the thin peak the children are now hanging off of like ornaments on a tree, and is standing against it, attempting to climb. It thumps its tail on the ground, its square head thrashing this way and that.

Henry grips the sharp edge of the pinnacle with one

hand while holding Button under his other arm. His knees wobble.

"I thought this was the very last thing we were supposed to do!" Jo's voice quakes in fear. She's clinging to the rock above Henry, and he can see the wavy bottom ridges of her shoes as she steps from one stone foothold to another. Pirate Girl is higher still, and Apollo is beneath him somewhere. Above them, the sky is as flat and gray as that stone, and below them, a great distance now, is that vast land of spikes and spires, and the jagged teeth of the Shadow.

"We had no choice!" Apollo calls upward. "There was no other way around!"

"Look! I got away faster than any of you! I'm not afraid up here at all," Jason Scrum brags. "I bet I'm related to a

*Or Something*

famous mountain climber or something."

"Follow me!" Pirate Girl shouts. "I see a ledge." At least, Henry thinks that's what she says. At that height, the wind whooshes around, and fright can be very loud in one's ears.

Henry reaches, reaches—ouch! Everywhere he grabs, there's a rock edge that jabs his thin, pale skin. He wraps his fingers around a jutting spike. Button is clutching Henry as tightly as he is clutching her. Now his foot stretches,

stretches from the ledge it's on to another, more distant one. Over this terrifyingly high canyon with a knife forest below, he's doing some sort of impossible feat of contortion.

*Impossible Feat of Contortion*

"You can do it, Henry! Stay still, Button! Only a few more steps!" Pirate Girl shouts. Henry quickly glances up. Pirate Girl is sitting on a flat overhang of rock, large enough for all of them. "I see a way down, guys!" she continues. "To a safe place, if you can only get here!"

Henry peeks down again, and, oh, it's awful. Apollo balances on a tiny wedge of stone. His fingers grip two small protruding rocks. His ankles and arms shake. Below them, spires upon spires zig and zag upward, like rows and rows of arrows ready to shoot from their bows. The Shadow cranes its endless neck to try to see them better. Above Henry, one of Jo's feet swings up to the spot where Pirate Girl stands, and then the other lifts, too.

"That was so scary!" Jo's voice trembles. She and Pirate Girl grab hands in relief and gladness.

"It's impossible!" Apollo cries, his voice full of tears. "I'll never make it! It goes on and on and on and on!"

"Don't stop believing, Poll! Hold on!" Jo says. "You can do it!"

As you can see, it's one of those *most* alarming times, where everything you say has an exclamation point. Button has gone completely quiet, as if she knows that a single wiggle might send them tumbling down into the vast canyon of knives. The ledge is just above Henry now, but it looks so far away. Fear mixes with all the terrible memories of recess—missed baseballs, and lost relay races, and smacks of the dodgeball against his thin legs. His confidence shakes, same as his hands, and his grip loosens.

"Henry, hang on!" Pirate Girl shouts. "You're almost here!"

Henry gathers every bit of might in his thin body and swings his legs until—all at once—he's up, and the girls are hugging him and Button both, and this would have been enormously embarrassing if he weren't so relieved.

"Plenty of room up here for me," Jason Scrum says, hopping neatly to the ledge and crowding them dangerously.

"Move over! Be careful!" Jo says.

"Stop taking up all the space, or we'll fall!" Pirate Girl says.

It's quite terrifying to look down from their rock shelf, and yet, Henry can't move his eyes from Apollo, who's still making his way from one jutting handhold to the next. He gets that feeling of doom about Apollo again, one that he had on their last adventure, when they were trying to change Rocco from a naked lizard back into a boy. It's like something awful is going to happen to Apollo sometime in the future. He has no idea what, but right now, he just tries to keep Apollo safe with his own concentration.

"Something wet is on me," the gerenuk says. "Blech! There it is again! How many times do I have to say it? NO WATER."

"He's right," Pirate Girl whispers to them nervously. "It's starting to rain! And that rock is only going to get more slippery."

"My hands," Apollo says. "I can't do it!"

The wind, well, it's bellowing in Henry's ears, and his eyes are locked on Apollo, but that's when something strange happens. Henry feels the drumbeat of courage, the bass note of bravery, the thrum of his own anthem coming from who-knows-where and who-knows-when. The important thing is, it rises within him with some sort of ancient clarity. *We can be heroes,* he thinks. *Even just for one day.* Henry gets on his knees.

"Henry, no!" Pirate Girl says. "That's too dangerous!"

But this is what a hero would do, or a friend, or a king, and so he reaches out his hand. "I'm right here, Apollo," he says.

Apollo takes Henry's hand, and Henry pulls. He pulls with

all his might. He pulls with more might than he even knew he had in his small body.

One of Apollo's knees reaches the ledge, and then . . . he's up.

"You made it, Apollo!" Henry wants to cry with relief and joy.

"Thank you, Henry. Thank you!" Henry can see tears in Apollo's eyes. Apollo hugs him hard. Henry wipes the sweat and dirt and old stardust from his hands.

"Henry! Henry! That was amazing," Jo says, and Henry's cheeks flush.

"It *was*, Henry! It was," Pirate Girl says. "Thank goodness, we *all* made it. We're here! And hey! Down there, the Shadow looks like a little toy."

Pirate Girl is right. From that distance, it seems almost harmless.

"And the way it's thumping its tail, it reminds me of you, Button, when you want to play."

Button gives Pirate Girl a doubtful look.

"But, guys, look over there." Pirate Girl shifts her focus from the vast canyon of spires from where they came, to the far side of the peak, out of sight until now. "Those bits of rock are practically *steps*! Pointed and jagged and horrible steps, but still. And do you see how *this* giant pinnacle and *that* outer edge form a barrier? If we can just get down, the Shadow won't be able to reach us."

"It's a long way, but we can do it." The thrum in Henry's head is fading, but he still feels that *ba-bamp* of courage.

"Let's hurry, before the rain really gets going and makes this limestone slippery as ice," Jo says.

"Wait!" Apollo says with excitement. "Do you see what *else* is down there?"

"Is it the wall? Or at least, the wall they're trying to build? It should be *somewhere* nearby." Pirate Girl squints.

"No one can see as good as you can in those glasses, Poll," Jo says.

"It's a lodge!" Apollo says. "A beautiful lodge at the edge of the Wilds."

"How wonderful!" Jo says.

Pirate Girl scrunches her face with suspicion. "Why in the world would there be a lodge at the edge of the Wilds? Who does it belong to?"

"*No one* comes here." The idea of a lodge makes Henry nervous.

"Maybe it's a warm winter home where we can rest for a minute before we go looking for the wall," Apollo says. "I'm exhausted."

"I'm just glad you can see the edge of the Wilds!" Jo says.

"I thought we might be lost in there forever," Henry agrees.

"Man, am I ever tired of being around you guys," the gerenuk says. "All you do is whine and complain, whine and complain, like a bunch of little babies." He moves his hooves around like a crying infant. "Wah, wah, wa—"

That's when it happens.

Something awful.

Something more awful than what has already happened, but less awful than what is coming. Jason Scrum loses his balance. He steps backward. He steps backward one inch too far, and before they know it, his hooves are scurrying madly midair, and he's disappearing from sight, vanishing down the far side of the summit, and there is a terrible, terrible gerenuk scream.

Here you must imagine the sound of—

Wait. That tragic cry is *impossible* to imagine. Something that horrible and distressing is too unbearable to describe. Even if you put many atrocious and ear-shattering noises together—the screeching brakes of a careening truck, the shriek of a dentist's drill, the wail that escapes your throat when your ice cream falls off the cone—it wouldn't be *this* sound, the kind that you feel even more than you hear. That scream whirls up inside Henry's whole body like a terrible cyclone.

"Jason!" Jo cries. "Jason, no!"

*A Terrible Cyclone*

## CHAPTER 20

# A Hazardous Trip Down

Pirate Girl holds her hands to her mouth in horror. "He can't . . ." She can barely speak. "He can't be all right, can he?"

Henry's stomach feels sick. "I don't think so," he says.

"Oh, oh, oh," Jo says. Tears gather in her eyes, and one drops off her nose, same as—well. Same as you-know-who just dropped off the you-know-what.

"This is so awful," Apollo says. "I mean, I was beginning to hate his guts, but I never wanted *that* to happen."

"I know," Pirate Girl says. "Same here. Thank heavens he fell on that side, though, and not . . ." That slurping and crunching sound now comes to each of their minds. Henry shivers.

"His poor parents!" Jo says. "And how are we ever going to tell Ms. Fortune? Instead of breaking the spell, we made things much, much worse. I'm sure Jason's parents would rather have had a stinky gerenuk for a son than no son at all!" She sniffles.

Pirate Girl is nearly crying, too. She has to wipe her nose on her sleeve before she's able to speak. "And . . . and what do we do now?"

The children look at Henry. Our Henry. Our thin, pale-skinned Henry with his knobby knees, who's still wearing his school clothes from the day before, clothes that are even shabbier now after a hungry Shadow and a magic cave and a forest of knives. Remember, too, that Henry is still up on that high ledge shelf, with the pinnacles below, and the pit-pat of raindrops beginning to fall. This is the problem when your grandfather is someone as wise and astonishing as Captain Every, the oldest spell breaker on earth. Sometimes your new friends look to you for answers when all you have are questions.

"We should make sure," Henry says, "that he, um, doesn't need help. I mean, that he isn't, or *is*, well, um . . ." Henry can't bear to say the word he's thinking. "And then . . . there is only one way out, and that's *through*." Oh, Henry. This sounds like what a coach might say to the team that always loses.

"Let's get off this slippery ledge before we *all* get impaled," Pirate Girl says.

*The Team That Always Loses*

147

With heavy hearts, the children make their way down each stone step. Henry has never felt so sad in his life. A crawl of guilt and badness overtakes him, too. *Poor Jason! I should have been nicer to him,* Henry thinks, taking one dangerous step down and then another.

"We should have been more patient with the bully," Jo says, dropping one foot and then the next into increasingly perilous territory.

"We should've?" Pirate Girl asks. She watches her feet, taking very sensible and slow steps.

"I feel just awful," Jo says.

"Me too," Henry says.

"And I don't see him anywhere," Apollo says. Henry's afraid to even look.

Finally, they've nearly reached the bottom of that horrid summit, and at the very moment their hearts cannot get even an ounce heavier, Pirate Girl stops.

"Wait," she says. "Do you hear what I hear?"

The whine is awful. Worse than a toddler after a long shopping trip.

"Where are you weirdos? Come untangle me," Jason Scrum cries.

## CHAPTER 21

# Quite a Tangle

H urry!" Apollo says, which is surprisingly easy now that they are at long last off that peak and on solid ground again.

"I can't believe he's okay," Jo says.

"Bullies are sturdy," Pirate Girl says, and sighs. This does seem to be quite true. So true that Button sighs out her nose, too.

"And thank heavens we're free of that Shadow," Jo says.

Henry couldn't agree more. What a relief! And here, on this other side of the Forest of Knives, at the outer edge of the Wilds, the land evens out, and the children find themselves in a wide, rocky area of yellow grasses and dirt, which goes on and on until it meets the beginnings of *another* forest. A more familiar forest. At least, a forest filled with the cedars and pines and spruces that the children are used to. Henry can spot the poky needles and mossy rocks and damp ferns that he's seen many times before.

"It's the forest on Rulers Mountain," Pirate Girl realizes. "This must be the far side of it."

For a brief moment—snap your fingers, because that's how brief—Henry feels almost happy to see a familiar landscape, even if it's part of Rulers Mountain.

But then he smells smoke.

He *sees* smoke.

He sees it roiling into the sky like an episode of *Rocket Galaxy* where Rex Xavier's ship is in trouble. Henry's heart *ba-bamps*. His tummy feels horridly wiggly, as if he's just eaten a bowl of Octopus Mondavi.

*Octopus Mondavi*

The smoke must be coming from that lodge somewhere in the distance. And this is terrible news, in Henry's opinion. Smoke means that it's not a great big empty lodge after all. *Someone* lit that fire. And the only *someones* anywhere near here are the evil people on Rulers Mountain, or maybe even Vlad himself.

"Smoke." Henry points.

"Oh no," Pirate Girl says.

"Maybe they have a fire going at that lodge. How cozy," Jo says. "I love that smell."

"Cozy?" Pirate Girl cries. "Only if you think Needleman or Vlad or Vlad's spies are cozy!"

"You don't know that for sure, Pirate Girl. We've never been on the far side of the mountain. You don't know who might be out here."

"The wall is somewhere nearby! Mr. Reese told us so! Who do you *think* is out here?" Pirate Girl says with alarm.

"I *wish* there was a wall nearby," Jo says. "But there's no sign of one anywhere."

"Wait. I see Jason," Apollo says. "He's waving his four hooves around in the air."

"Would you people hurry up?" the gerenuk cries. "You're the slowest weirdos in the world."

"Remember when we felt so sorry for him back there?" Jo says.

"Wow. I'm already despising him again," Pirate Girl says. "That was fast."

"He just keeps on being who he is." Henry sighs.

Now they all see the gerenuk. He's stuck on his back, like an upside-down potato bug. His hooves point skyward, and his big alien eyes bulge. He looks completely unharmed, except for a strange red string wrapped around his legs in jumbled knots.

"Oh no. Look at him! What a mess," Jo says.

"What is that stuff?" Pirate Girl asks.

"Yarn. Red yarn," Apollo says. "My mother used some just like it to make a beautiful holiday craft."

"That's so strange. Why would there be yarn out here?" Pirate Girl asks.

"Where have you guys been?" Jason Scrum complains, waving his hooves around and making the tangle worse. "One minute, I was standing way up high, and the next, I was floating through the air. And then these"—he tries to point to his oversized ears, knotting the string even

*A Beautiful
Holiday Craft*

further—"began to spin like a helicopter, and this"—he wiggles his rump, indicating his tail—"rotated in a circle, and I was like a human whirligig, floating downward and away from those spiky trees. I have no idea how that happened."

"It could take us *hours* to untangle him," Jo says. "And there's no wall in sight, and it's already afternoon. The celebration of love is in *one day.*"

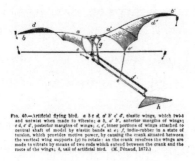

Fig. 48.—Artificial flying bird. *a b c d, a′ b′ c′ d′,* elastic wings, which twist and untwist when made to vibrate; *a b, a′ b′,* anterior margins of wings; *c d, c′ d′,* posterior margins of wings; *c, c′,* inner portions of wings attached to central shaft of model by elastic bands at *e; f,* India-rubber in a state of torsion, which provides motive power, by causing the crank situated between the vertical wing supports (*g*) to rotate; as the crank revolves the wings are made to vibrate by means of two rods which extend between the crank and the roots of the wings; *h,* tail of artificial bird. (M. Pénaud, 1872.)

### How That Happened

"Don't worry, Jo." Pirate Girl whips her pocketknife from her vest and holds it in the air. "I'll have him out in no time."

"And then we'll hurry and find the wall," Henry says. "And we'd better *really* hurry. We're completely out in the open."

Pirate Girl is slicing bits of string and holding other bits of string in her teeth. "I don't understand, though. The wall should be right here," she says, though it sounds like *I ont unerhan, oh. The wall ould be ight ere* with her teeth biting down on the yarn.

"Ow, you nicked me!" the gerenuk screams. "Now I'm bleeding everywhere."

"I barely touched you," Pirate Girl snarls. "And quit wiggling, or it will happen again."

"Stop making such a racket, too," Jo scolds. "Do you want us to be found?"

"The string . . . ," Apollo says, peering through his wondrous glasses. "It goes on and on. Look."

"It does seem to," Henry says, though he couldn't tell you for sure, even with the hardest squinting he can muster.

"Maybe we should follow it north a little, toward that lodge we saw," Jo says. "I'm sure whoever lives there could help us."

"I don't know about that," Henry says. He's not sure at all. Safety is never the first thing he imagines, even on a regular day.

"How do we know who will open that door?" Pirate Girl says, agreeing with Henry. "We're so close to Rulers Mountain, and that supposed wall."

"It looked like a very nice place from up above," Apollo says, agreeing with Jo. "It would be great to sit by a fire for a bit and have something warm to eat."

"There," Pirate Girl says to Jason Scrum, who stands on his hind legs and shakes off the last of the string.

"When my mother finds out about this, you're all going to be in big trouble," he says.

"You're welcome," Pirate Girl says, sticking her knife back into her vest. "Do you know how hard it was to get you out of that? It was like you were lassoed by the best cowgirls."

"Come on, guys," Apollo says. "Let's at least look at the lodge. Anything

*The Best Cowgirls*

would be better than standing out here where anyone can see us."

Henry tries to stay hopeful as he and Button follow behind Apollo and Jo, with Pirate Girl trailing, and the gerenuk bounding ahead of all of them. In the distance, he sees a winding river, the river from the cave, he's sure, which has somehow made its way under, around, or through that Forest of Knives summit. And he sees the lit windows of the lodge growing larger. Button sniffs the whole length of that string. The fur on the dog's back is up, which sends chills down Henry's arms. Then again, he's still in his thin shirt, dampened by rain, and the hole in his shoes has gotten larger and a pebble has snuck inside, and maybe that's the patter of a shower again, darn it, and—

Henry nearly bumps into the back of Apollo, who has stopped quite suddenly, and then Pirate Girl nearly bumps into the back of Henry, and Jo has stopped, too, her eyes wide. They are nearly at the enormous log lodge. But this is not what causes Apollo to fly his hands to his mouth in terror.

"Jason, no!" Apollo cries.

## CHAPTER 22

# The Wall

The gerenuk's head is down, and his horns point forward, and one hoof paws the ground. His eyes have taken on a focus the others have not seen in him as a boy or as a beast. And what he has in his sights: two enormous caribou, with enormous antlers rising majestically toward the sky. Enormous times enormous times two caribou— Jason is in serious trouble.

"Gerenuks are very territorial!" Apollo says, his voice high and squeaky with alarm. Jason grunts, and steam escapes his nose, and Button runs to hide behind Henry's knees.

"Eyaaaaw!" Jason shrieks, his horns storming ahead of him. Jo hides her eyes. Apollo cringes. Henry peeks at the scene the same way you do during a movie that's too frightening to watch.

The caribou charge. There's the clicking-clashing clatter of horns locking with horns. It sounds a bit like Rex Zavier's sword when he attacks the Rebel Army in an exciting episode of *Rocket Galaxy*.

Only, the lock seems to be permanent, because Jason Scrum can't move. The caribou antlers have him completely paralyzed. His feet paw the ground, but he can't go anywhere. He's in one of those humiliating positions where you're forced to say uncle.

*One of Those Humiliating Positions Where You're Forced to Say Uncle*

"Are you crazy?" one of the caribou yells to Jason, before unlocking him and stepping back. "Is this any way to move through dangerous territory unnoticed?"

"Wait," Pirate Girl says. "He talks?"

"*She* talks," the caribou says.

"Both males and females of the caribou species have antlers," Apollo says. "Though males have slightly larger—"

But this is no time for caribou facts. "So sorry," Pirate Girl interrupts. "It's just kind of hard to tell."

"Brenda is much better looking than I am," the other caribou says.

"Oh, Eddie," Brenda says. She blinks her lashes toward him, and he blinks his lashes back. "Still. This is a dangerous way to behave right by the wall."

"The wall?" Henry says.

"I don't see a wall," Jo says.

"Where?" Apollo asks.

"Right here!" Eddie says, putting his large velvety nose down toward the ground.

"Wait. All I see is a piece of string," Pirate Girl says.

"Shh!" Brenda says, her eyes alarmed. "He's very sensitive about it."

"He?" All at once, dread begins to creep across Henry's skin.

Eddie's caribou lips mouth the words *Vlad Luxor*. Jo's eyes go wide.

"'Bad cold sore'?" Jason Scrum guesses. Clearly, gerenuks are terrible lip readers.

"I don't understand," Pirate Girl says. "I mean, this can't be—"

*The wall?* Eddie mouths.

"'The gall'?" Jason Scrum says.

"I'm afraid it is," Brenda says.

"But it's nothing like he said it would be," Jo whispers. "Nothing at all."

Apollo is stunned. "He said it would be magnificent and amazing and high and strong and—"

"And that it would keep everyone out and him in, because *others* were awful and a terrible emergency, and—" Pirate Girl says.

"And it's—" *A piece of string,* Henry mouths. He's just as astonished as everyone.

"Well, we must pretend it isn't," Brenda says. "We must pretend it is a big stone wall where there—of course—can never be a wall." Brenda rolls her caribou eyes.

"There can't? Not even with the most evil magic?" Jo asks.

"Apparently not," Eddie says. "Vlad can't seem to make it happen. Trouble with this, trouble with that! And then, something else, too. Every time they put another brick in the wall, set a stone on a stone, or erect *any* sort of structure, the strange and ancient Wilds actually quake and shiver, sending the bits and chunks in all directions, quite like Mother Nature herself is putting her foot down."

"Oh wow," Pirate Girl says. "The Wilds are full of mysteries."

"So, instead of brick or stones or steel, Vlad's workers set up this *string*, this friendly red yarn, with a tiny, tinkly bell on one end, which alerts us when anyone crosses the, um—" Eddie clears his throat. "*Wall*. We heard the little *ting-ding* just now and had to come and investigate."

"It's our *job*," Brenda says.

"Your job?" Henry asks. It's a strange career for two caribou.

"We patrol the territory. We're guards."

"Guards? But you look like friendly caribou," Apollo says.

"We weren't always caribou. We were forest rangers, and that was our house." Eddie points one hoof toward the magnificent lodge. "We were there to protect and guard the Wilds, not this silly . . . I mean, *magnificent* wall." He winks.

"We didn't even know anyone was out here protecting the

Wilds," Jo says.

Brenda sighs. "For such an important profession, it's surprising how little attention it gets."

"And *no one* is doing it now," Eddie says. "You-know-who doesn't believe in protecting the Wilds or the seas, or our very earth. Poof! He turned us into caribou, and turned our ranger station into his vacation home."

"Why caribou?" Pirate Girl asks.

"We were *rangers*, and caribou are technically *Rangifer Tarandus*, I suppose. Likely a built-in part of the spell. Knowing Latin seems unlikely for—" *Vlad Luxor,* Brenda mouths.

"'Third world war'?" Jason Scrum guesses.

Henry doesn't want to ask what he must ask next. "His vacation home? He's not *here*, is he?"

"Oh, *please* say he's on Rulers Mountain, ruling." Jo crosses her fingers on both hands.

Brenda laughs, her big caribou nostrils moving in and out in the cold air. "He spends much less time doing *that* than anyone thinks. Right now, he's fishing in that river, just around the bend, while everyone else bustles inside, getting ready for the big dinner tonight."

"He *is* here," Jo moans with dread.

"For a big dinner? Tonight?" Henry asks. His heart begins to thunder, and even on this cool fall day, sweat starts gathering in his pits.

"Do you remember when Best Farriver used to have those

large, elegant parties, where people would come from far and wide to dine with the esteemed leaders of the province? Well, you may be too young, but take my word, they were gracious occasions," Eddie says.

"But you-know-who," Brenda continues, "he wants freshly hunted game from the Wilds, eaten with your hands, and elaborate costumes from days of yore."

"If Vlad Luxor is here . . . does that mean Needleman is,

*Elaborate Costume from Days of Yore*

too?" Pirate Girl asks.

"Well, yes, of course, but lucky for you, *all* of Vlad's people are very busy today," Eddie says. "Inside, making preparations for a feast. Outside, with their nets and bows and arrows. Thankfully, they're far north of here and stay at the outer edge of the Wilds. Otherwise, you'd have surely been spotted by now."

"When we heard the tiny tinkle of alarm at the border, we came as fast as we could. Of course, we weren't anticipating an attack by *him*." Brenda points with a big shaggy hoof to Jason Scrum.

"We're so sorry," Henry says, because he's quite used to apologizing for things he hasn't done.

"We're here to help you in any way we can. We know who you are," Eddie says.

"You do?" Henry can hardly believe it, the way that he's gone from being practically unseen to being known by strangers like these two kind, shaggy caribou.

Brenda whispers again now. "Only forest rangers and *spell breakers* with important business would risk traveling through the Wilds. What with all the tangly plants and evil spirits . . ." She makes a pretend-scared face at Eddie, and he chuckles a deep, husky caribou chuckle.

"But it's not a spirit at all!" Apollo tells them, turning white with the memory. "The Shadow is *real*. It's terrifying! A horrific crocodile-like monster! It charged at us!"

"It *charged* at you?" Brenda says, her voice full of disbelief.

The children look at one another. "Well, maybe not *charged*, exactly . . . ," Pirate Girl says.

"Um . . . ah, well," Jo says, "it walked toward us, and then, when we saw it again, it tried to climb, and then its tail . . ."

"Thumped? Like a puppy who wants to play?" Brenda asks.

"A very large and scary puppy," Jo says.

"Well, some crocodile monitors are very aggressive and some are shy. You can't lump them all into one group! You have to get to know them individually, just like people," Eddie explains. "Jenny—she's rather playful and quite intelligent."

"Jenny?" Henry asks.

"Yes, Jenny, Jenny!" Brenda says somewhat impatiently. "Eight-six-seven-five-three-oh-nine. Is that her correct specimen number, Eddie? Or is it three-oh-*eight*?"

"No, you're correct. If I recall, eight-six-seven-five-three-oh-eight is our screaming hairy armadillo," he says. "Jenny is as sweet as a summer day, though it's much better if people *think* she's a frightening evil spirit. Crocodile monitors used to be hunted and skinned alive to make drums."

"Drums! How awful," Jo says.

"It's sometimes very dangerous to be an *outer* or an *other*, as I'm sure you already know," Brenda says.

"The Shadow is a regular, spectacular animal!" Apollo can hardly believe it.

"A *weird* animal," Henry says in wonder.

"And her name is Jenny." Pirate Girl grins. "I love the Wilds more and more every minute."

"Well, we're sure you have some important business in

the area, whatever it may be," Brenda says. "And we're here to help you in any way we can."

"Because you need us to turn you back into forest rangers?" Henry asks.

"Oh, no." Eddie looks at the children with his warm brown eyes. "We actually quite like being caribou. We want to help because it's *the right thing to do*."

You can imagine how these words feel to all the children, especially Henry. Even though they've just heard some very relieving information about the Shadow, that lodge is up ahead, and Needleman is nearby somewhere, let alone Vlad himself. Those words are like being tucked into a soft feather bed, and served a wonderful warm cup of Deep Cocoa with Plumps.

"The important business that we're here for . . . it's to help *him*," Pirate Girl says, hooking her thumb at Jason, who has found a tree to munch on.

"Him?" Brenda says, with the calm shock only a caribou could muster.

"He's not a gerenuk at all. He's a boy," Apollo explains.

"We have to walk him on the line between good and evil, falling on the side of good. Can you help us with that?" Jo asks. "We thought the line was the wall."

"There's no *wall*, but there *is* this line." Eddie kicks the string. "And he certainly has fallen—right smack onto the side of evil, though."

"Ugh, you're right," Pirate Girl moans.

*We've already failed,* Henry thinks, and when he looks at Apollo, he sees that same thought on his face. Henry could cry. It's been a very arduous journey, and the day is getting later and longer, and it's all been for nothing. Dismay—that awful mix of disappointment and lost hope—sinks into his heart. And then, well, things rapidly get worse.

Button, who's been quiet this whole time, tucked behind Henry's legs, begins to growl. A very serious and threatening growl. The fur crawls up her back like a ridge of unmowed grass.

"What's wrong, Button?" Henry asks.

*Ridge of Unmowed Grass*

"Shh!" Brenda whispers. "They're coming! They're *much* closer than we thought." She paces and paws the ground, and Eddie huffs and lowers his horns, and then . . .

Oh, you may want to hide your eyes, because this is frightening *and* terribly sad. Large, scary men, Vlad's men, emerge from the nearby edge of the Wilds. One has a net over his shoulder, and one has a rope at his hip. But the third . . . he's carrying a platter with Mr. Reese strapped on top.

*"Chee chee chee!"* Mr. Reese cries. *"Chee chee chee!"*

"Shut him up," the man with the net says.

A tiny apple is shoved into Mr. Reese's mouth, and now he looks ready for the oven. His eyes bulge in alarm.

What's even more terrible—Henry can see that the pockets of Mr. Reese's lovely apron are filled with nuts. Innocent nuts! Mr. Reese must have gone for breakfast after all, and perhaps got lost. Henry feels a weighty rush of guilt and sorrow. He'd misjudged Mr. Reese, and now look.

"Mr. Ree—" Jo cries, and Pirate Girl reaches out an arm to stop her. Those men don't know that this particular squirrel is Vlad's former left-hand man, the traitor Mr. Reese, who can *talk*.

Jo's eyes fill with tears. "We have to help him!"

But sadly, the children won't be helping anyone.

"Well, well, well," Needleman says. He adjusts his cuff links and lifts his chin in victory. "Look what we have here. Little brats who have wandered too far from their mommies. Lost in the forest with no trails of bread crumbs to follow home. No one to kiss your boo-boos and cut your meat in tiny pieces and sanitize your precious fingers with special goo. What a tragedy." He tsk-tsks meanly. "Maybe Vlad will have his fresh meat after all."

CHAPTER 23

# Capture

In an instant, the spy with the rope makes a single loop around all the children and cinches it tight. The rope cuts into Henry's stomach, and he feels Apollo's elbows jabbing his sides, and Button is squished in the middle of them. The gerenuk is still munching the top of a nearby tree, and Brenda and Eddie have suddenly gone full-on caribou, nostrils sniffing the air, eyes staring blankly around, pretending that animals are not the brilliant creatures they are.

"Let me out of here, you monster!" Jo yells, kicking at the spy with her boots and jabbing her fingers toward Needleman's face, poking him in the eye.

"Ow! My eye! You hideous little dirtbag!" Needleman cries as she reaches to scrape her nails down one of his arms. "You nasty, silly, frail little girl!" He smacks her hands away.

"I'll show you a frail little girl," Pirate Girl snarls. "Hit me

167

with your best shot! Fire away!" She scoots and twists and manages to sock him right in the center of his guts.

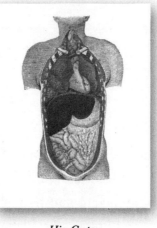

*His Guts*

"Oof, blrrr." Needleman stumbles. Henry gets in a blow to Needleman's knees. "Wrap their arms, you idiot!" Needleman grunts to the spy, who is doing his best to wind another loop around the squirming, fighting children and one twisting dog.

"LET US OUT OF HERE!" Apollo screams.

"Are you nuts?" Needleman hisses, grabbing Apollo under his one free arm and pinching hard. "Be quiet! Our esteemed HRM is just up the river! Do you know what he'll do if he sees that some very particular children have jumped his wall and made their way into his territory? And do you know what he'll do *to me* when he finds out that you exist? Shut your mouths immediately, until I can shut them permanently!"

Right then, in a move Juana Azurduy herself would have been proud of, Jo reaches out again and manages to yank two single hairs on Needleman's arm, which, as you know, can be extraordinarily painful. "YEEEEOWWW!" he screams.

As is generally true, it's a very *unquiet* scream. And that's when things go from bad to worse. A voice, that skin-crawling and terrifying voice, comes booming across the land.

"Needleman! Is that you? Where have you gone?" Vlad Luxor shouts. "I want to catch a big marlin! I want to put his body on a wall and his chewy flesh on a cracker! You know I like success at whatever I do!"

The children go still. They stop squirming and fighting and protesting, because true evil can halt you right in your tracks, like a boot smashing a bug.

Henry's afraid to look. He knows Vlad Luxor is coming closer, though, because that voice gets louder. "A giant fish on a hook!" he shouts. "With bulging eyes and a huge, wriggling body, and a mouth gasping for breath!"

Henry can feel the other children trembling next to him. He feels the ribbed cave of Button's chest go still. They've all turned cold with terror. He can't imagine what horrible thing might happen next.

Henry peeks and sees the swoop of Vlad Luxor's hair, and

his hangy jowls, and the dull flash of his yellowed teeth. He strides toward them, slowed by a pair of high, rubbery hip waders, which make an unnerving *squeak squeak* sound as he walks. "Needleman! Where's my hat! Don't I need a lucky hat? Every fisherman has a lucky hat that makes you catch fish!"

*A Lucky Hat That Makes You Catch Fish*

The rope cinches tighter. Jo lets out a little moan of dread. In a moment there he is, Vlad Luxor, right in front of them. Henry can feel Vlad Luxor's hot breath, which smells like canned mussels and yesterday's coffee, and he sees the hard yellow shells of Vlad Luxor's fingernails on his red fleshy hands. Henry's sure he has only a few seconds left before he's turned into something horrible, so he closes his eyes and hopes his grandfather knows how much he loves him.

"What's this?" Vlad Luxor says, kicking Henry's shoe with the toe of his fat rubber boot. "Who are *you*?"

Henry opens his mouth. He wishes and wishes he could use his voice in some strong way, but no sound comes out.

"A group of . . . workers," Needleman says. "Loyal workers. Youth for Vlad! Here to serve."

"Yes, yes, of course. Wonderful." Vlad Luxor lifts his globby chin and angles his head to get a better look at them. "Wait."

And then he reaches out. He grabs Henry's narrow face and tilts it up so that Henry is oh so horribly staring straight at him. "They look familiar," he says. He lowers his brows menacingly. "They look like *particular* children, Needleman. I can't put my finger on it." Vlad's hard nails jab into Henry's cheeks as he turns Henry's head this way and that to study him.

"Oh, no, no, *no*! Not particular at all!" Needleman is speaking rapidly, and he's gesturing like a windmill at top speed. "Just a few of your many young fans. Here to lend a helping hand at the magnificent festivities tonight."

Vlad Luxor looks directly into Henry's eyes, and Henry has no choice but to look back. And this is very difficult to explain, because you have likely never seen such a thing yourself, but Vlad Luxor's eyes look dead, as if there is no true human being there at all, and even his voice seems flat and wrong and false, as if anyone real inside his body has gone missing. And yet, Vlad Luxor blinks, and Henry can feel the *blop blop* of Vlad Luxor's pulse in his fingers, and his putrid breath puffs in and out. Henry shudders; a chill goes down to the center of his bones, because Vlad Luxor is like an empty ghost who is still very much alive.

"Well, then. Get happily to work for me!" he says. "And get me that hat, Needleman. I'll be down at the river catching a marlin big enough to mount on my wall. Dead decorative animals show my glorious power."

Vlad's hip waders *squeak squeak* as he turns, and the ground shudders. Henry can still feel the pressed indentations of Vlad Luxor's fingers in his face.

"Get them out of here!" Needleman hisses. "Lock them up. I'll deal with them as soon as I can. And no funny business from you, brats. Every move you make, every breath, every blink, every burp—I'll be watching you."

And with that, in a tangle of feet and a huddle of bodies, the spy shoves them toward that lodge, where the smoke curls like a dark question mark toward the sky.

## CHAPTER 24

# The Surprise in the Trophy Room

T he spy pushes and wrangles the bundle of children through the tall doors of the lodge. Inside, a huge wood hall leads to an even more immense room with an enormous fireplace crackling with a warm fire, which leads to *another* immense room with the largest and longest table you can imagine. There are delicious smells, too, and workers are bustling about, and it's all somewhat wonderful even though it's an awful place, because the children have been out in the cold for two days and one long night and haven't eaten anything since they had the last of Apollo's Luscious Lime Pockets. Beside him, Henry hears Pirate Girl's stomach growl.

The spy shoves them through each room, grumbling and muttering, *Not here, not here,* because there are people everywhere, polishing and tidying, gathering platters and trays, and setting the table with large iron plates and tall iron goblets. He heads to a pantry and opens the double doors, and Henry silently hopes they'll be hidden there.

Inside, Henry spots food beyond his wildest imagination: Oyster Jams and Jells. Beef Valentinos and Pork Valentinos and even Tofurkey Valentinos. Choco-Blintz Nuggets, cans of Peach Romblé and Brown Sugar Radish, and every other splendid thing you can think of, along with a yucky something or two (a large jar of Black Licorice Guzzles, ick). He sees four entire rows of canned vegetables. What extravagance!

Unfortunately for the hungry children, one of Vlad's workers is inside the pantry, perusing a shelf of boxed mixes for Vanilla Mond-du-fait. So, the spy shuts the doors quickly and

*What Extravagance*

shuttles them forward, past a large kitchen, where Henry can hear the sounds of sizzling butter and things frying. He sees one of the chefs open the oven and slide in a very familiar-looking platter. And this is difficult to say, and even harder for the children to witness, but those tiny, creepy feet are familiar, too. Jo lets out a sob.

"Mr. Reese!" Pirate Girl whispers.

"Oh no!" Henry whispers back. His heart breaks. The chef cranks the dial to the highest heat.

Now the children and Button, still tied together in their awful huddle, are thrust and jostled down another great wood hall. The spy opens a set of doors into a magnificent bedroom with high ceilings, where—ah, Henry can't get a good look in. Someone's there, too, so the spy moves on. Finally, he pokes his head into another magnificent, high-ceilinged room with no one in it. The spy shoves them inside and locks the door behind him.

They're alone again. At least, they think so.

"It's . . . a library," Apollo says. "Or at least it *was*." All the shelves have been emptied of books and are filled with trophies instead, decorated with golden Vlad Luxors in every size, and Henry can see the words FIRST, and CHAMPION, and WINNER, and BEST engraved on their plaques. There's another fireplace in here, too, and it's lit and warm, but hanging above the orange, crackling fire in the stone hearth, there's a chilling sight.

*A Chilling Sight*

Jo's noticed it, too. "Don't look above the fireplace," she says.

"Oh, that's awful," says Pirate Girl, looking above the fireplace.

"Don't look on the wall across from it, either," Henry says, which of course makes everyone turn and crane their necks in that direction. A deer head on one wall, and an elk head on another—Henry could cry for a million reasons.

"As if this day couldn't get worse," Apollo says.

But then something astonishing happens.

"Those poor children," the elk on the wall says.

"All roped up like cattle," the deer on the other wall says.

Henry is so shocked that he nearly steps on Jo's foot, and Button is so startled that she begins to growl, and then Pirate Girl says, "They speak!"

"Talking heads! How awful," Jo says. "How did this happen to you?" It's just like Jo to think of others even when she's in dreadful trouble herself.

"We have no idea!" the talking elk head says. "The last thing I remember, I was standing in the lovely shade of my forest home. Suddenly, I found myself in another part of the world, in a beautiful house, and I said to myself, 'This is not my beautiful house!' I looked over and saw that deer on the wall, and I said, 'That is not my beautiful wife!' I asked myself, 'How did I get here?'"

"Oh dear," Jo says.

"Exactly," the deer head says. "The same thing happened to me."

"And now *you* have arrived," the elk head says. "And I am guessing, although I don't know for sure, that you are the spell brea—"

"Shh!" the deer head commands, causing the elk to shut his lips, pronto.

"Quite right," the elk head says. "With only a head, I should be thinking much more clearly! You are, I assume, the children we've heard . . . *whispers* about?"

Even as that tight rope digs into Henry's skin, and even as they are held captive in a madman's lodge near the edge of the Wilds at the far side of Rulers Mountain, it's quite remarkable to think that even the *animals* of the Timeless Province know about them.

"We are." Apollo nods solemnly.

"We're here to help a bully gerenuk," Jo says.

"A bully, truly? Well, I'm assuming you have your reasons and it's important business, or you wouldn't have put yourself into the great danger you're in now," the elk says.

"We *have* to get out of here. Needleman will be back any minute, and there's no telling what trouble the gerenuk will be getting into, especially with those hunters all around! And we've got to hurry because it's getting quite late and tomorrow is Jo's mother's celebration of love," Henry explains in a rush. For a moment, it's like he read that book that's advertised in the back of *Amazing Stories* magazine.

*That Book That's Advertised in the Back of Amazing Stories Magazine*

"We *can't* miss the celebration!" Jo cries. "My mom and Becky will cancel the whole thing if I'm not home soon."

"And we'll certainly miss it if Needleman . . ." Pirate Girl's hands are bound, so she makes a face like she's being strangled, her tongue lolling out the side of her mouth.

"We have to, um, put our heads together and think about what to do. With apologies to you both," Jo says to the heads.

"No apology necessary," the deer says. "The first order of business seems to be to get you free from that rope."

"That seems completely and utterly impossible," the elk says.

"It's not. I'm already working on it." Pirate Girl has somehow wiggled her fingers into her pocket, and she's clutching her pocketknife. "The saw blade is really small, and it's hard to cut anything at this angle . . . ," she says, grunting with effort.

"You're amazing, Pirate Girl," Henry says.

"If anyone can do it, you can," Jo encourages.

"If we manage to get free, what then?" Apollo says. "I'm sure that door is locked, and there's only that one small window up there, with bars across it. How will we get out?"

"We *have* to find a way," Pirate Girl says, sawing with all her might.

"Why is our HRM so intent on keeping others out and inners in?" the elk moans. "No one can get through those bars."

"We'll find *some* way out. But this place is crawling with workers," Jo says.

"And as soon as the party begins, there'll be even more." Henry can't imagine how they'll escape, let alone escape without being seen.

"The party must be starting soon. It's gotten noisier and noisier out there. And just before you arrived, *that* was delivered. We have no idea what it is. It took three workers to muscle it in." The deer rolls her eyes toward an enormous wardrobe shoved against the wall.

"This is a very thick rope," Pirate Girl moans. "But I think I almost—wait! It's just about throu—"

"Needleman!" Vlad Luxor shouts, rattling the knob of the door at the exact moment that the rope slides from their bodies onto the ground. "I need you! I'm bored of fishing and I need a marlin NOW. The guests are beginning to arrive! Needleman, are you in here?"

CHAPTER 25

# The Children Use Their Skills

O h, it is the worst possible thing to happen, because the rope clatters down, and then there's Vlad, popping into the room, causing a terrible commotion of fear and panic in their bodies. The talking heads go silent.

"Who are you? What are you doing in here?" Vlad booms as his chest expands to terrifying proportions. "My most special room is always locked! No one is allowed. And what is that nasty, messy rope doing in my beautiful, precious trophy room right before my magnificent party?"

"We're Youth for Vlad," Apollo squeaks.

Every spongy, magical, useful corner of Henry's brain seems to have dried up and gone dark. He opens his mouth, and at first, nothing comes out. But then: a miracle. An idea. An idea plus bravery.

"We were just putting up this wall, sir."

"Wall?" Vlad cocks his head, the way a bird does when he's suddenly caught sight of you.

Henry lifts the rope. "This powerful wall. To keep *others*

out. Out of your trophy room. A lock didn't seem like enough for such a magnificent and marvelous place of tribute to you, sir."

"Ah yes," Vlad says. His big chest relaxes. "The more barriers, the merriers, I always say. Carry on."

With that, he exits, and all the children exhale in relief, and even Button sighs through her nose, but then the door opens again.

"Wait! Is that what I think it is? The wardrobe of splendid, stylish costumes has arrived!" Vlad says. The children suck in their breath again. "I told them to lock it away in my most special room, since tonight, *I myself* will be the most glorious, shining trophy!"

No one dares make a move. Just when they thought they could breathe a sigh of relief, they're unsafe again—a situation Henry is already familiar with. He knows that you sometimes have to make bravery last, the way you suck on a candy rather than crunching down. Vlad strides over to the wardrobe, flings open the doors, and removes hanger after hanger and trunk after trunk of elegant and somewhat flashy clothing—velvety vests and lacy leggings and satiny suits. He *hmms* and *hahs* his approval as many furs and minks and leathers begin to pile up. The deer and the elk heads blink with fear, as if the worst hasn't already happened.

With a great weight of clothes over his arms, Vlad exits. The lock clicks into place again.

"Whew," Jo says.

"It's times like this that I am glad to be an other and not an inner, even if we are locked out," Henry says.

Pirate Girl nods. "I know what you mean."

"We have to get out of here, and fast," Apollo whispers.

"We have a chance, now that Pirate Girl freed us with her wonderful pocketknife," Henry says, and Pirate Girl beams.

"But how?" Jo asks. "I just wish Brenda and Eddie knew where we were. We need someone *out there* to help us *in here.*"

"It sounds like we have a window of opportunity, since Needleman has to catch a marlin. After all, marlin live far out at sea, not in rivers, and they're fast, too, sometimes swimming sixty-eight miles per—"

"*Window* of opportunity!" Pirate Girl interrupts Apollo. "It's our only way. Maybe we can wave our arms to show Brenda and Eddie where we are."

"That window is high," Apollo says. "And there isn't even a chair in this room to stand on."

"What about those trunks and suitcases in that wardrobe?" the elk says. "You could stack them! They're practically a *ladder.*"

"You're right!" Jo says, hurrying toward it. "Let's see. Each of these trunks is about ten inches, and that window is about seven feet high, and . . . Seven times twelve, eighty-four inches, divided by ten equals eight and a bit less than a half, minus the head and shoulders of our climber . . . So that's . . . seven trunks!"

The children run back and forth, stacking the suitcases, and Button runs back and forth, too, in encouragement and excitement. The trunks rise up, up, up, reaching as high as

*Practically a Ladder*

the children can manage on their toes and with their outstretched fingers.

As they stand back to look at it now, their ladder seems quite high and exceedingly wobbly.

"I'll go," Henry says.

"Are you sure?" Pirate Girl asks.

"I'm the smallest." Henry carefully climbs from trunk to trunk. The higher he goes, the more rickety and swaying the suitcases get.

"Hold on to them!" Pirate Girl barks. "The trunks are slipping this way and that!"

"We're trying!" Apollo says.

When he glances up, Henry worries that there aren't enough trunks for him to reach the ledge, but of course, Jo has calculated perfectly.

"Whew!" he says. "I made it."

"Yay, Henry!" Pirate Girl says. "Great job, Jo! Your math skills are the best!"

"Thanks, Pirate Girl!" Jo says, pleased. "What do you see out there, Henry?"

Well, he sees the last rays of afternoon light shining toward him, turning the tips of the evergreens golden and the edges of the sky a glowing orange. Even more important, though: "I see tower workers in fancy costumes, hurrying around."

"Are there lots of guests from faraway places and important dignitaries?" Apollo asks. "Like when Best Farriver was our RM?"

"I don't think so," Henry says. "It's just the same old tower workers we've seen before, wearing different costumes."

"Do you see Brenda and Eddie anywhere? Or Jason Scrum?" Pirate Girl asks.

"Or worse . . . *Needleman*?" Jo asks.

"I see . . . I think I *might* see Brenda and Eddie, or else two large and shaggy armchairs. And maybe a gerenuk with bulgy eyes facing this direction, unless that's a very tall coatrack."

"Try to get their attention," Apollo suggests.

Henry waves his arms around, which is a courageous thing to do on those wobbly boxes. "It's no use. They can't see me."

"Open the window and shout," Apollo suggests, and because Henry's used to following all orders without protest, he wiggles his fingers toward the latch and unhooks it, and then shoves and shoves with all his might until the window is up, the cool air blowing in.

"Wait. We can't do that," Henry says, at the very same moment that Pirate Girl and Jo and even the elk and the deer shout, "No!"

"They'll hear us! The tower workers! Needleman! The spy!" Pirate Girl reminds Apollo.

And then Apollo says something Henry has already known for a long, long time. "Ugh! It's so hard to keep your head on straight when you're hungry. With apologies," he says to the talking heads.

"No problem at all," the elk head says.

"But we *must* find a way to get them to see us," Jo says. "Getting help seems like our only hope."

"Hey!" Henry says. Once again, an idea and bravery mix together to form something powerful. "I remember something from my *Ranger Scout Handbook*, sixth edition. The way everyday objects can help you survive in the wilderness! Your shoelaces can be a fishing line. Your socks can filter water. And your eyeglasses can help you start a fire, or—"

"Signal someone!" Apollo says. "Signal, by redirecting the sunlight using the lens. I know how to do that! Should I try to throw my glasses to you, Henry?"

"Oh, I don't think so," Henry says. "Your glasses are way too important, and they might break. And I'm not sure if I remember exactly how to signal."

"We'll switch spots, then!" Apollo looks more confident and excited than he has since the moment Henry first saw him with his new glasses. Henry makes his way down the boxes, and Apollo makes his way up, which is, of course, quite a bit more nerve-racking to watch, given Apollo's athletic build. The suitcases smush and squash and tip. But Apollo is up there, holding on to the ledge with one hand. With the other, he removes his frames.

"You can also use your glasses for a fishing hook, or to pry grubs from a log," Henry says, because once you start being helpful, it can be hard to stop. Apollo is concentrating, though. He aims the one lens toward the beam of sun and then adjusts the angle.

"Can they see you?" Jo asks with great worry and anticipation.

"Any shiny object should work. As a beam of light hits a prism, the beam slows, which changes the angle the light moves, and then the light bends again as it exits . . ."

Honestly, this is quite confusing, though Henry gets the general idea.

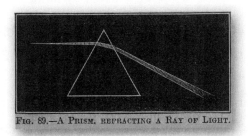

FIG. 89.—A PRISM, REFRACTING A RAY OF LIGHT.

*The General Idea*

"Jason is facing us, and I'm aiming it . . . almost . . . there. There, it's right in his eyes!"

"What's he doing? Does he see?" Jo asks.

"I wish I could wear my glasses *and* use them," Apollo says, with new appreciation for his specs. "Because it's hard to tell for sure. But it looks like he's batting the light away. Kind of like he's whining and complaining and rubbing his eyes."

"Ugh! If only it were Brenda and Eddie seeing the signal," Jo says. "They'd know what it was. They wouldn't think only of themselves."

"Wait," Apollo says. "Brenda's turning around. Or, maybe that's Eddie. It's hard to tell who is who from this distance. But, yes! They're turning! They're looking!" Apollo begins to wave his arms. "They see me! Here they come!"

CHAPTER 26

# Perfectly Thin

Well, the great big clock in Henry's head really begins to tick now. It is not a *tick, tock* any longer. Now it's a *TICK, TOCK, TICK, TOCK*. He can hear the bustling sounds outside the door, meaning the lodge is filling with workers, and that Needleman will be back any minute, and that night is coming and so is the day of Jo's mother's celebration of love. Apollo is waving his arms and saying excitedly, "They're coming! They're coming!"

"I love your glasses, Apollo! I love your glasses so much!" Pirate Girl cries.

"I do too!" he says with great glee. "I do too!"

Even from below, on the floor where the children and Button stand, they can see the horns and the strange alien-like eyes of the gerenuk up on his hind legs, peering in the window.

"What are you guys doing in there? Well, that looks nice and cozy and warm, while we're stuck out here in the cold!" Jason whines. "Hey! Stop shoving me off this rock,

188

you caribou! I can't see!" Somehow, he makes even those words—*you caribou*—sound like an insult, even though those magnificent creatures should only be looked at in awe.

*Awe*

"Don't worry, children," Brenda says, her calm *Rangifer Tarandus* voice drifting through the window and down to them. "We'll have you out in no time."

"We just need to . . ." Eddie grunts. In order to reach all seven feet up, the caribou have climbed atop a large, flat stone below, and Eddie's antlers are locked onto one of the bars, and Brenda's are locked onto another, and there's ferociously loud grunting and huffing and snorting, such important and meaningful noises that Henry's sure they'll be heard.

"Oh dear," says the elk head inside.

"Exactly," says the deer head.

But Button begins to turn circles of excitement, and

Pirate Girl grips Henry's sleeve, and Jo's cheeks begin to redden not from the warm, crackling fire but from the joyful thought of escape, because it's happening. The bars are bending, bending, bending.

"Ah!" Brenda sighs. "That's it. That's as far as I can go."

"Yes, me too," Eddie says. Their big nostrils strain from effort.

"Well, let me—" Apollo says. He tries to stick part of his body through, and then he tries again another way, and then he attempts an arm and then just a head, but it's quite clear—there's no way he'll fit.

"We won't be able to get through," Pirate Girl sighs.

"You *have* to get through," Brenda says. "Or at least one of you does. There's an extra key hanging on a hook in the kitchen. A skeleton key. It opens all the doors of the house. If it's still there, of course. That's where *we* kept it when the lodge was our home. I would get it myself, but hooves are not hands."

Eddie's big shaggy face pops into the window frame. "Brenda's right. Someone needs to get outside, walk back into the house, retrieve the key, unlock your prison, and set you all free."

*Not Hands*

"I don't see how it's possible," Jo says. "That is a very, very small hole."

"Way too small," the broad-shouldered Apollo says.

But Henry knows something about himself, and he knows it very well, because it's one of the things that the bully Jason Scrum has teased him about again and again. "I'm small," Henry says. "I'm thin and small enough to fit."

"Do you really think so, Henry?" Jo says.

He looks at the hole and at his narrow arms and legs. "Yes. I'm *perfectly* thin."

"You are, Henry! You *are* perfectly thin!" Pirate Girl says, and Henry's chest fills with gladness.

Apollo climbs down the suitcase ladder, and Henry prepares to climb up.

"Wait," the elk head says.

"Wait just one minute," the deer head says.

"You can't let them see you," the elk reminds him.

"At least not like that. What about those costumes, right in the wardrobe? There seems to be all sorts of sizes and varieties of things." The deer rolls her eyes that direction.

"They'll think you're a visitor to the party!" says the elk head.

"They're right!" Pirate Girl says. "And if Needleman sees you, he might not realize who you are, at least at first."

"I guess it's true." Jo smiles. "Two heads *are* better than one."

## CHAPTER 27

# The Most Wrong Words

As you can imagine, it's quite difficult to squeeze oneself through the tiniest hole while also wearing a somewhat roomy and elaborate costume of velvet and satin. Henry has a difficult moment where he's stuck half in and half out, and where it looks like the ground is a long, long way down. Jo makes a quick calculation and suggests a twenty-degree-angle slide to a caribou's back, minimizing the distance Henry has to fall. When everyone is in place, and he manages to slip and eke his body out into the evening air, falling just so onto the shaggy back of Eddie, Henry feels as thrilled as if he is Harry Houdini himself, performing the great milk can escape.

*Houdini Himself, Performing the Great Milk Can Escape*

"Well done!" Eddie says, dropping to his knees so that Henry can slide off. Now that he's outside, it's much clearer what great danger he's in, because there are workers everywhere, all in extravagant costumes, some playing strange instruments from a different time.

Jason Scrum, per usual, is only thinking about himself, munching heartily on the upper branches of a nearby tree, but Brenda nudges Henry forward with her squarish nose. "Go. Hurry! Get the key on the hook hanging right by the kitchen door."

*Strange Instruments from a Different Time*

"Your friends are counting on you," Eddie adds, which doesn't help Henry's nerves.

"Just act natural," Brenda suggests, which is exceptionally difficult when you're wearing fancier clothes than you ever have in your life, let alone when you're in great danger. Acting *unnatural* would be better advice, because Henry needs to be more of the things he isn't usually: daring and bold.

He takes a big breath and moves his thin little legs toward the open lodge doors, and that's when a huge figure suddenly fills the entryway. Henry feels a *whoosh*—the cold blast of an arctic wind—as Vlad Luxor appears. His paunch presses against his velvet waistcoat, and his belly splurches over his lacy breeches, and he's wearing the gold brocade and garish jewelry of evil kings of the past.

*The Gold Brocade and Garish Jewelry
of Evil Kings of the Past*

"Welcome, dignitaries from foreign lands!" Vlad booms, though of course Henry sees only the crowd of scary-faced workers, now making their way into the lodge. Almost immediately, Henry's caught among them, flowing forward like a salmon forced upstream. Vlad claps the backs of workers and *ho-ho-hos* in heartiness and cheer. Then he leans back on his heels and waits for the praise and admiration the workers must say before he lets them inside, like a secret password.

"I bow to you, your honor," one worker says.

"I give you my life, Great Emperor," says another.

Henry's stomach churns with the nearness of yuck, but also with terror. He tries to think of his grandfather, Captain Every, who faced and conquered Avar Slaven, a dark and evil man from another time, and he thinks of his *friends* (the word is still magical to him), who are desperately waiting for him in that locked room.

Henry summons his courage. He's sure Vlad will recognize him. But their hideous HRM never truly sees anyone or anything else, of course. He's only looking for glorious reflections of himself, even if they're lies. Same as in that mirror on the day this terrible story began.

Now Vlad stares down at Henry. His globulous neck wobbles. He claps Henry on the back of his velvet coat, making his thin frame shudder. He waits for some magical words of praise, but Henry's mind has gone as blank as Vlad's eyes.

"Yes? Go on." Vlad's flat gaze is rapidly shifting to something quite sinister, more and more so the longer that Henry is frozen there with his mouth hanging open.

"I . . . I . . ."

Well, what happens next is awful, and may be the saddest moment in this story, so if you must pause to honk your sorrow into a hanky after hearing it, go right ahead. But poor, poor Henry—his voice, which is always such a problem, truly fails him. He's in a state of shock with Vlad standing in the doorway like that. And what pops out of his mouth are the most wrong words, the same words he's required to give every day under similar circumstances, when a tyrant stands at the door of his very own home every morning.

"I . . . I . . . love you," he says.

Ah! Those most beautiful words given wrongly . . . Almost immediately, a shame and a horror and a deep regret drop over Henry. His face turns a dreadful red. Even so, Vlad beams, and moves his gaze onward, to the person behind our grief-stricken boy. And of course, Henry has no time for the curling badness in his tummy, either. He has to rush through the huge hall, and the enormous room with the fireplace, his eyes skirting back and forth, watching for Needleman.

Which way to the kitchen? It's difficult to remember, or even find his way, with his head spinning from upset, and with the workers rushing around, carrying large platters of food and setting them on the big table in the dining room, where Henry is now. The large iron chandelier above the table is lit with twenty candles or more, which twinkle their reflections in the windows turning dark with twilight. The goblets shine, and the food smells unbelievably good, and Henry must hurry, because people are standing behind their chairs, waiting for Vlad to come inside and sit down.

The velvet of his sleeve brushes past the velvet of other sleeves as he hurries out of there, following the sounds of clattering—pans and pots, dishes and silver. Left, right, left again, until he's in the busy kitchen with the huge stove and the counters filled with dishes under silver domes, the scary worker chefs in white click-clicking their long sharp knives and jostling their sizzling pans.

He is through the door. Now he only needs to find the hook next to it. That's where the keys are supposed to be. Henry is so close. It sounds so simple: Grab the keys, and then make his way down the great wood hall to free his friends.

But the hook, the hook! Where is it?

There is no hook.

There's only a framed oil painting of Vlad Luxor wearing a sash that reads FRENCH CHEF. When the forest rangers lived in that lodge, there was a hook and a key, but not now.

Now there's only Vlad and more Vlad. A prison of Vlad with no way out.

The last of Henry's hope is gone. He doesn't know what to do. He is full of despair, and then—

"*Chee chee chee!* CHEE CHEE CHEE!"

There's a creepy, awful scratch of nails against silver from under one of those domes, a shivery *scritch-scritch*. Henry lifts the curved lid off the platter, and now he finds something wonderful and heart-lifting, because there is Mr. Reese, looking like he's been out in a rainstorm, lying on a bed of lettuce, a sprig of parsley on his tummy.

"Mr. Reese!" Henry exclaims with joy.

"Shh!" Mr. Reese says.

"You're not cooked!"

"The chef decided at the very last moment that squirrel is best served *carpaccio*."

"Carpaccio?"

"Raw, with vinegar and oil." He shakes drops of vinegar from his bonnet-clad head, and casts off the parsley. "Get me out of here!"

Mr. Reese is quite soggy and also heavily salted and peppered, and it is always extraordinarily shivery to touch, let alone—ugh—pick up a squirrel, but Henry snatches Mr. Reese off the platter and hides him in his velvety waistcoat. Henry has no idea what to do next, since there are no keys. But one of the chefs is turning around now, so he must do *something*. He *has* to get out of there.

Henry's brain scurries madly. Much to his horror, right as he remembers his grandfather's words that *a plan will present itself*, a back door flings open, when he didn't even know there was a back door. And there is Needleman, grasping a large salmon. For one brief second, Needleman looks quite exhausted after a day of fishing and attending to evil, but then he spots Henry and his eyes alight, and the salmon spurts from his arms and slides across the metal countertop.

"Well, well, well. Henry Every. Now, this is what I call the catch of the day."

## CHAPTER 28

# A Most Fortuitous Turkey Leg

Henry tries to escape. Needleman is slowed briefly by the fact that the salmon blops from the counter onto the floor, and he must step over it, causing him to slip and slide as the chefs turn and grab at the fish, and at a dish of Chicken Candelabro with Peas, too, which is threatening to fall. There is the general pandemonium one sees whenever there is a chase scene in a busy kitchen in any film or television show. It is all quite true, Henry understands, the way the dishes begin to fly and crash as one weaves and darts around, and the way there is suddenly an asparagus in mid-air, and a madman with a butcher knife chasing you.

He dodges one chef wielding a spoonful of butter, as well as a worker entering the kitchen with a tray of freshly emptied bottles of Sparkling Vrés Fondoo. There's the unnerving *slice-slice* sound in the air of Needleman wielding that blade.

Henry flees, but there is nowhere to go, and unfortunately,

very, very unfortunately, he makes an unwise move. It's so unwise that if you saw him do it, you'd jump up and down and yell, *No, Henry, No!*

He dashes into the pantry. The pantry, with no escape. And so of course Needleman has him trapped, and Henry huddles in the far corner, trembling, his heart beating hard. Here's when you might see someone in an exciting film hurl cans of peaches or Celery in Cream Water, but in real life, Henry's too scared to do anything like that. It's also difficult to be athletic wearing velvet, and inside Henry's coat, Mr. Reese is squirming rather unnervingly, because Henry has buttoned him in quite tightly.

"I'd rather have all of you at once, but I'll take one," Needleman says.

Henry holds his breath. He squinches his eyes and pulls his shoulders up around his ears in protection, and Needleman has that knife in the air, and he is coming toward him, and—

"Needleman!" Vlad booms. "Needleman, where are you? It's time to start dinner, and I want every chair filled before I sit! There is an empty chair, Needleman!"

Henry peeks out of one eye. Needleman has turned to face their hideous HRM, but that knife is still in the air.

"NEEDLEMAN! What are you doing? Are you trying to KILL ME?"

"Oh, no, no. No!" Needleman rapidly brings his arm down

to his side. "Of course not! I'm—I'm preparing to carve the large and magnificent turkey! Right, yes! The one in the very center of the table!"

"Well, get on with it, then," Vlad says, his satin rustling. "And you know what piece I want, don't you? The one piece I can eat with my hands, like the kings in days of yore?"

"Yes, sir, of course I do!"

"Say it to me."

"The giant turkey leg, sir."

"Chop-chop," Vlad says, and claps his hands to speed Needleman along, and we should pause here to reflect how very awful those same words could have been, had Vlad not interrupted Needleman at that very moment.

*The Giant Turkey Leg*

"Mfhh-hhhph," Mr. Reese says from inside Henry's extravagant coat. He manages to pop his head up, and, oh, it is beyond yucky, a thousand times beyond, to have a squirrel so close to him, let alone one doused in vinegar. Still, Henry does his best to stomach it, because Mr. Reese *cares* about them, and they care about him, too. "Don't just stand there!" Mr. Reese shouts.

Now Henry does something that, you know already, would be terribly, terribly wrong in any other circumstance, but which is understandable and forgivable and even wise in this one, when he and his friends are in danger and trying to fight great evil. Henry grabs a few Carbo-Cal Zowz bars, both in chocolate and peanut-butter-and-chocolate, and shoves them into his pockets. He rushes out of the pantry, and then the kitchen, now quite in disarray, which is a fancy word for a gigantic mess. Henry heads—

"WHERE ARE YOU GOING?" Mr. Reese shouts. "Are you out of your mind? The front door is THAT way!"

Henry heads down the great hall toward the locked trophy room. The locked trophy room for which he has no key.

"Everyone else is inside and can't get out," he tells Mr. Reese.

*"Aargh!"* Mr. Reese tosses up his little paws in frustration. "What am I going to do with you children?"

Henry ignores him, reaching the shut trophy room door, pounding both as loudly and as softly as he can. "Pirate Girl! Jo! Apollo! Button! I'm here! I'm here!"

"Henry!" Jo says in great relief, and it's this great relief that makes it awful, so awful to do what he does next— confess his failure.

"It wasn't there!" he says. "The hook was replaced with a painting of *him*. I couldn't find it."

"Oh no!" Apollo says. "Oh no. It's over."

"Don't cry, Jo," Henry hears Pirate Girl say. He's filled with such sadness, and hopelessness, and despair.

"Try the knob, at least!" Mr. Reese says.

"Is that Mr. Reese?" Pirate Girl says.

"I smell carpaccio," Apollo says.

Henry rattles the knob, but no, it's locked all right.

"Psst."

Henry stops. He's sure he just heard someone in the hall.

"Psst. Down here."

It's a bearskin rug, laid out on the floor. The eyes of the bear's head blink.

"Oh no! I'm so sorry. I didn't see you down there." He steps off of the black fur, splayed flat.

"Thank you," the talking bear head says.

"What happened to you?" Henry asks.

"Some psycho killer. What is it?"

"What is what?"

"It! The *it* you are talking about."

"What's going on out there, Henry?" Pirate Girl's voice is muffled behind the door.

"It?" Henry says, ignoring Pirate Girl for now. "A key. The key. To open that door. My friends are locked inside."

"I hear a man," Jo says.

"Your *friends*?" He squints his eyes, which you wouldn't think was possible from a bearskin rug, but actually is. "You aren't . . . I can hardly believe it! It's an honor to be stepped on by you! Spell br— Oh my. Well, you must get out of here at once!"

"That's what I was saying. We can't get out."

203

"Of course you can. There's a key right underneath me. People are always hiding keys under the most obvious things: the welcome mat, the largest rock, the flowerpot in the far corner of the patio . . ."

"Under *you*?"

"Yes, yes! Get it and go! Go, run! Get out of this terrible place!"

*The Flowerpot in the Far
Corner of the Patio*

## CHAPTER 29

# Something Magical

Wisely, the children are already ready for their escape, dressed in their own elaborate costumes to better hide from Vlad's workers. Pirate Girl has chosen a broad-brimmed velvet hat, jeweled cape, and some fine leather breeches, worn over her pirate clothes. Jo is in a brocade gown of mulberry and gold with an embroidered cap, and Apollo is sporting green satin knee-pants, striped socks, and a white shirt with puffed sleeves, covered with a fur-lined, calf-length vest, his backpack over his shoulder. Button's collar is green velvet with multicolored emblems, and a carved buckle. The children only have time for a rushed but relieved reunion with Mr. Reese, the hastiest of thank-yous to Henry, and a hurried goodbye to the kind but very thoughtful heads.

"Run and hide!" the bear hide says.

"Oh dear," the elk says.

"Exactly," the deer says.

The children and Button and Mr. Reese race as fast as

one can in elaborate layers of clothing, galloping and tripping down the hall toward that open door, but of course Needleman can hear their shoes tap-tapping across the floor, and he can see the swish of a fancy skirt and the bright flash of a satin-clad leg as he stands at that large table with a carving knife in his hand. Needleman's face reddens when he spots them, and he glares straight at Henry. Even in that costume, it's like Needleman can see right through him.

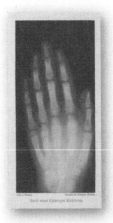

*Right Through Him*

"Dark or light, Congressman?" Vlad Luxor shouts. "Take your pick, or have both. And what about you, Councillor? My generosity is boundless. Needleman! Carve and slaughter more quickly!"

Needleman catches the attention of one of his spies. He gestures toward the children, sending a clear message with his menacing stare and one raised eyebrow.

But the open doors are finally in front of them, and Button is racing ahead. The spy begins to give chase. Now that they're out into the night, the dark and cold fall night, Henry runs as fast as he can, and so does Jo, and Apollo, and Pirate Girl. Jason Scrum suddenly joins them, and even he understands that this is no time to be foolish. He runs like a gerenuk, while Mr. Reese scurries as rapidly as a squirrel heavy with condiments can.

And then, right then, something magical and wonderful occurs. These are the things that can happen when good people (or caribou) do what's right simply because it's right. Brenda and Eddie are waiting, their shaggy, huge selves bent down at the knee so that the children and Button and even Mr. Reese can climb atop them. Henry and Pirate Girl swing their legs over the massive body of Eddie, with Button snug tight between them, and Apollo and Jo do the same on Brenda, with Mr. Reese sitting firmly in the back. And then, Henry gets to do something magnificent, absolutely wondrous, which is, he gets to take ahold of those strange and majestic antlers. Pirate Girl loops her arms around Button and Henry, and on Brenda, Jo grips the creature's great horns, as if she's Juana Azurduy in the cavalry, and Apollo sets his arms around her.

And then, in the moonlight, the caribou take off. They take off so fast and strong that no spy or worker or evil at all could catch them. Because caribou have their own wonderful weirdness, a weirdness that they use right now. As

Apollo can tell you, caribou can run almost fifty miles an hour, and swim long distances. With their large hearts and odd habits—like clicking their knees so that they can find each other even in the deepest darkness or the most blinding blizzard—they can travel and travel over every terrain for hours on end.

And when Henry finally gets to rest his cheek against Eddie's warm and shaggy neck as he gallops as wild and mighty as nature intended, his nostrils sending white puffs into the night air, his muscles pumping in the moonlight, the will and the kindness and the goodness of the great beast charging forward, Henry realizes something important. Weirdness is beautiful, as he already learned. But weirdness is powerful, too.

## CHAPTER 30

# A Weighty Decision

It is very, very difficult to keep their eyes open. Even Henry—who usually stays awake and alert for danger—is struggling. It has been a terribly exhausting and frightening few days, but now he's safe on that large, splendid creature, and he's snug and warm in clothes that are heavier and lovelier than he's ever worn before. All of that can make you quite drowsy, and even almost at peace. When he looks over at Jo, though, her hands are still locked tightly on Brenda's horns, and her eyes as wide-open as she can keep them.

"How much longer?" Apollo asks. His head slumps.

"Miles and miles," Eddie shouts. "We can't cut through the Forest of Knives, pardon the pun, heh-heh. So we must travel the entire outer edge of the Wilds. We'll be there by morning, if we keep going."

"Morning!" Jo says, brightening. "The celebration of love is at the golden hour of twilight. We can still make it."

"Indeed we can. A celebration of love should never be missed," Brenda shouts back.

As much as Henry and the others would love to rest, they *have* to keep going. They have failed Jason Scrum, who is still a gerenuk, and so many awful things have happened for no reason that they can see, and Ms. Fortune will be heartbroken. But they can at least make it back in time for Jo's mother and Miss Becky.

The caribou keep plodding forward, following the winding river and the route around the edge of the Wilds that only forest rangers know about. The stars twinkle like the glowworms in the limestone cave, and Henry can smell the dreamy dew of evergreen, and pines sleepy with sap, and that solemn fragrance of wet earth that means it might rain.

But gerenuks cannot run forever like caribou can. Jason Scrum is slowing down, and Apollo keeps drifting off, nearly slipping from Brenda, and Henry can hear Pirate Girl's tummy rumbling badly with hunger. He has the Carbo-Cal Zowz bars, both in chocolate and peanut-butter-and-chocolate, in his pocket, but as you can imagine, it's too difficult to try to hand them out and eat them on the back of a galloping beast. Clouds drift in, and the moon seems to swim, and it is so dark and deep in the night that it's past the very latest hour you can ever remember staying up.

*The Very Latest Hour You Can Ever Remember Staying Up*

"Stop," Jo finally says. She says

it loudly and calmly, but also with sadness and defeat. "Stop. We need to eat. We need to sleep. We won't make it there by morning. We just won't."

Brenda and Eddie slow. "We'll make it if we keep going," Henry says.

"We can't keep going," Jo says.

Apollo nearly tumbles from Brenda in exhaustion. And now a plink of water drops onto Henry's nose.

"Rain, dear," Brenda says to Eddie. Eddie snickers.

"Shall we head to the clover? Under the shelter of the eucalyptus?" Eddie asks, and Brenda bobs her big head in agreement.

"Jo, are you sure?" Henry asks. He wants to cry.

She nods. "I'm sure."

"But your mom might cancel it all if we don't get there soon," he says.

"I know," Jo says.

Brenda and Eddie kneel, and the children slide off onto a soft mattress of clover. Jason Scrum collapses in sleep right there, as does Mr. Reese. Henry hands everyone a Carbo-Cal Zowz, and Button runs to the edge of the river and laps and laps at the cold, rushing water. The children stumble to the river, too, to drink from cupped hands, and then they lie down next to the warm bodies of the caribou until their eyes close.

## CHAPTER 31

# An Astonishing Forest and an Awful Confession

Henry's dreams are so strange. His mind tumbles with images of their narrow escape, and Needleman with that knife, and the upcoming celebration of love, and the terrible yucky feeling he still has after giving Vlad Luxor the best words you can ever give. He dreams of a particular set of yellow crocodile eyes watching them in the darkness, though maybe that's not a dream at all. He dreams of women in white dresses and planets and moonlight and rough, frightening terrain.

*Women in White Dresses and Planets and*
*Moonlight and Rough, Frightening Terrain*

But when he wakes again to a new morning . . . Well, it's as if they've been transported to another land entirely. Henry sits up, still wearing his elaborate and rather stylish costume. In the darkness, Henry couldn't see what surrounded them, but now he does: trees with trunks in rainbow colors, and plants with flowers that are clear as glass. And then, a little distance away, he spots the square head of the enormous Shadow, peeking from a dark corner of the colorful landscape. Those yellow eyes are staring right at him, and Henry's heart speeds in alarm. But then, he swallows his fear, remembering that it's wrong to believe untruths about people or animals, even crocodile monitors. He gives a shy little wave. He swears he hears an enormous thump and feels the earth tremble before Jenny disappears again. It's like they've had a silent, private conversation that he'll never forget.

Jo awakens and sits up, too, wiping the grass from her brocade dress. "Look at those trees! Red and yellow and blue and orange."

"Purple and green and aquamarine!" Pirate Girl says sleepily.

"And glass-like flowers. I've never read about those." Apollo stretches, and then rises to his feet to investigate, with Button following behind him.

"They don't even look real," Henry says.

"Rainbow eucalyptus," Brenda tells them, and then yawns a large caribou-sized yawn.

"And skeleton orchids," Eddie says. "After a rain, the petals are so thin that they turn transparent as ice. Magical, aren't they? Well, I love a rainy night. Such a beautiful sight."

"It certainly did drizzle, though I feel quite dry," Brenda says.

"Me too," Henry says. Their heavy clothes have kept all the children warm and snug. Jason Scrum scowls and shakes like a dog after a bath, though, and Mr. Reese jiggles the water droplets from his bonnet.

"My lovely hat is coming in rather handy," he says.

"This forest!" Apollo shouts. "It looks a painting made by Vincent van Gogh."

*A Painting Made by Vincent van Gogh*

"And the flowers on those trees . . . They're like bright pink tassels," Jo says.

"Beautiful, beautiful weird," Pirate Girl whispers to Henry, and he nods and smiles, because it's all most *definitely* beautiful, beautiful weird. Rainbow trees, and glass-like flowers . . . a private, shared moment with an unusual beast . . . Well, it's so stunning and spectacular that it makes Henry want to wrap his own weirdness around himself like a fabulous and valuable coat. A unique and cherished coat. A coat he might wear with pride every single day.

"I'm starving," Jason Scrum whines.

"I'm hungry, too," Apollo says.

"There are quite a large number of nuts and seeds and edible fruits all along that riverbank," Brenda tells them, the way a forest ranger would.

"If someone with hands wants to come, I'll point them out, given that I now have an unfortunate wealth of such knowledge. When I was a man, I dined at La GreenWee." Mr. Reese twitches his tail, which is still rather spiky from dried vinegar and oil.

"I'll go," Henry says. He leaps up, and Button zooms to join him, because Henry is her person.

"I will, too," Pirate Girl says. Her velvet hat is off, but she still wears the jeweled cape like a warm fall coat.

"Do keep an eye on the squirrel. Jenny *is* a carnivore, after all, even if she has no interest in *you*," Eddie tells the children. "Rodents are her favorite, especially mice and rats."

"Hmph! Do I look like a rat to you?" Mr. Reese grumbles. "Lately, everyone thinks I'm a meal!"

"We'll keep our friend safe," Pirate Girl says, and pats his little head.

Jason Scrum has taken off, and is chomping his way along

the top of a ridge of trees. As they head to the river, Henry is already thinking of pages 148 to 152 of the *Ranger Scout Handbook*, sixth edition, which show all the astounding things in a forest you didn't know you could eat.

*The Astounding Things in a Forest*
*You Didn't Know You Could Eat*

This beautiful morning has all the excitement of adventure without any of the terror, and so Henry almost skips toward the water. When he glances over his shoulder, though, his cheer vanishes. Henry sees the look of worry and sadness on Jo's face. All at once, the heaviness of their failed mission returns, and so does the bad feeling that's been troubling Henry. His stomach begins to ache.

"Are you all right, Henry?" Pirate Girl asks.

"It's the morning of the celebration of love. And Jason Scrum is still a gerenuk," he says.

"I know," she says. Button yips and circles a scowling Mr. Reese as Pirate Girl and Henry pluck several lilly pillies and wombat berries. "It's awful, everything we've been through for nothing. Is that all, though, Henry? You seem sadder than even all of that. Sadder than even that huge amount of sad."

Henry peeks at Pirate Girl. He feels embarrassed and even ashamed to admit what happened back when he passed through the lodge doors, when he gave the most magical and precious words to Vlad Luxor. He doesn't even want to confess something so horrible. But Pirate Girl is waiting patiently for him to answer.

"I said something bad to Vlad Luxor," he whispers as he kneels by the river.

"I'm glad. You should have said lots of bad things to him. But I'm relieved he didn't turn *you* into a bushy-tailed rodent."

"No, I mean a *good* something bad. Something . . ."

"What, Henry? It's okay. You can tell me."

He can barely speak. "I told him the most perfect, magical three words. So that I could pass by safely." Henry's face turns a deep red. He hopes they'll still be friends after a confession like that. But Pirate Girl's eyes are only full of sorrow, and she seems to know what three words he means without him having to explain.

"Oh, Henry," she says.

"I should never have done it." He blinks back tears.

"No way," she says. "No way, Henry! You did what you had to do. We should never feel bad for what we do to survive a bully."

He stares down at his hands.

"I once told Ginger Norton that she was pretty so she'd stop being mean to me. *Before* I sent her down that icy hill on a cardboard sled."

"You did?" Henry can hardly believe it. Pirate Girl always has a way of understanding him like no one else seems to.

"Yeah. Gross. But it's *all* brave, Henry."

A weight lifts inside of him, like the anchor of his own personal ship. He even smiles.

"Come on," she says.

Mr. Reese's apron pockets are stuffed full of tree buds and pinecone bits and even a mushroom or two, and Button enjoys a delectable squash and several asparagus tips, and Pirate Girl and Henry and the other children have a wonderful breakfast of wild fruit, and it's all juicier and more filling and delicious than many breakfasts that Henry and Button have had at home. The caribou forest rangers manage to find their favorite reindeer moss and lichens, and Jason Scrum chomps with his usual bad manners on a strawberry guava. And, thank heavens, Jenny does not emerge again to devour Mr. Reese. The children eat quickly, though. The minutes are ticking by, and there is still the slightest but narrowing hope that they'll arrive in time for the celebration of love to go on after all. Scrumptious juice is trickling down their faces, and Apollo wipes his mouth with the back of his hand, and Jo is tying her shoes, eager to leave, when suddenly Eddie freezes, his large nose in the air.

"What is it?" Brenda asks.

"Smell," Eddie says.

And with that, Brenda makes an alarmed snort, and Eddie paws the ground, and a terrible scent fills the air, a new stink beyond the more familiar one of the gerenuk.

"Pee-yew!" Pirate Girl says, and plugs her nose.

"Our apologies," Brenda says. "But this is what happens when caribou warn each other."

"Warn?"

"A predator is coming. We smell him," Eddie says. "We can smell him for miles."

"Hurry, children," Brenda says.

## CHAPTER 32

# A Difficult Parting

They quickly tidy their camp, like any good Ranger Scout or wilderness visitor, and then they yank Jason Scrum from his reverie of leaves. The children and Button and Mr. Reese climb on the backs of Brenda and Eddie.

"How about we take the shortcut?" Eddie asks Brenda. Henry can feel the hot puff of his breath. "You know, the one that passes the little waterfall, and then the big one, and then the one that's especially high?"

"Don't go chasing waterfalls, Eddie. Stick to the river we're used to. It's a little farther and will take more time, but I'm sure whoever we smelled back there *will* take the shortcut."

"Farther and more time?" Jo says sadly. When Henry looks over at her, he sees that her eyes have filled with tears.

"Farther and more time?" Jason Scrum whines from the back. "I miss my mommy."

"I'm sorry, Jo," Apollo says.

"Me too," Pirate Girl says.

"Me too," Henry says. His heart is breaking.

"It will *also* take them quite a distance from the main entrance of the Wilds in Hollow Valley, where they said they left their bikes," Eddie says.

"Ugh," Pirate Girl says. "It gets worse and worse."

"Safety first," Brenda says, and that's when they hear it: something awful. Something terrifying—a pig-like grunting, and then a horrible, cackling cry.

"I know you're in here somewhere, you little brats!" Needleman's voice winds and lifts through the tree branches of the Wilds.

"Oh no! Needleman! I thought he would *never* come to this place!" Apollo says.

"He must want to find you very, *very* badly." Eddie shakes his caribou head with the deepest concern.

"I promise you, you have not seen the last of me!" Needleman shouts.

"Go!" Brenda commands, and the caribou charge and rumble forward.

Henry leans on Eddie's neck. It's a dewy fall morning, and the large orange sun has only just risen in the sky, and the air chills Henry's cheeks, the only part of him not covered in the heavy velvet of that costume he still wears. As the caribou bolt through the forest of rainbow eucalyptus, there's the delicious minty-sneezy-green smell of the leaves, and even at their rapid pace, Henry spots a carnivorous caterpillar eating a moth whole. A huge dragonfly speeds by their noses in a blur. Jo sees an unnerving spider, whose back seems to be decorated with delighted eyes and a smiling mouth. Apollo makes frightening eye contact with a feral pig.

*Frightening Eye Contact with a Feral Pig*

They ride for a long while, and morning turns to midday. They emerge into a field of curly, swirly, and coiled cork-screw grass, where they rest oh so quickly to drink from the curved green bowls of the wine-cup plant before riding on. They travel through a narrow valley-like corridor, and a secret wooded tunnel. And then finally, finally, as the clock ticks toward late afternoon, Henry sees something—an opening. A curve of light, a clearing. The caribou slow until they stop, and so does the gerenuk. Through that clearing, Henry sees the broad sky, and it's as if the sun has filled the space with warmth and with the golden light of fall.

"We are so sorry, children," Eddie says. "We know this journey has taken much longer than you'd wished."

"It's okay." Jo's voice wobbles.

"And we're so sorry, too, that we have to leave you here, in this inconvenient spot, but this has been the safest exit from the Wilds," Brenda says. "The very farthest corner of Huge Meadow is *always* the safest and most hidden place."

"The farthest corner of Huge Meadow? We'll *never* get home," Jason Scrum whines.

"Wait. What did you say?" Jo asks.

"That we're sorry. Leaving you here, so far from your bikes," Brenda says. "Since we're at—"

"The farthest corner of Huge Meadow?!" Jo and Henry and Pirate Girl and Apollo all cry at the same time.

"Is that where we are? Really? It's so hard to tell," Apollo says.

"Yes, we had to go a great distance across the very hidden outer edges of the Wilds that zig and zag under the valley and up again, but I can assure you, we're some distance from where you left your—"

"That's wonderful!" Jo exclaims. She slides off Brenda and flings her arms around the caribou's thick neck. "That's absolutely wonderful! *Thank you.*"

Eddie kneels, and Henry and Pirate Girl hop off. Even though Jason Scrum is still a gerenuk, Henry is filled with joy and excitement and relief. "This is where the celebration of love is supposed to take place," he explains to the caribou, "if it's still going to happen."

"Enough about the blasted celebration of love!" Mr. Reese complains, throwing his creepy squirrel hands in the air.

"Certain children need to sort out their priorities! Like keeping safe from madmen! Like turning squirrels back into the fine gentlemen they truly are!"

"The exit of the Wilds. It's through there?" Jo asks, pointing to the curve of light.

"Right through there," Brenda says. "This is where we say goodbye."

"But . . . can't you come with us?" Henry says. He somehow hadn't realized the caribou would stay behind, and Henry suddenly can't bear the thought that all of them won't continue on together.

"Oh, that would be quite nice if we could," Brenda says politely. "But we love the Wilds. It's our home, and it's still our job to watch over it every way we can."

"So . . . this is where you leave us?" Pirate Girl says.

"It is." Eddie nods his large square nose.

*"Thank you,"* Henry says. It's one of those times that those words aren't big enough. He puts his arms first around Eddie and then Brenda, and he sets his cheek against each of them, and then all the children are hugging the caribou while being careful of their great antlers.

Finally, the caribou turn and head back into the tangled, magical Wilds. And that's the last you'll hear about Brenda and Eddie. Nothing more than you've been told already. The children can barely see them now. But still, here they are, waving Brenda and Eddie goodbye.

## CHAPTER 33
# An Electric Event

I n spite of the weight of their failure—coming home with the same gerenuk they left with—stepping from the Wilds is a big moment for all of them, the children *and* Button, and their hearts feel like five enormous balloons, ready to lift.

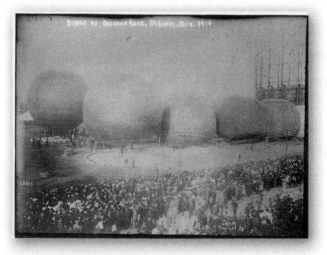

*Five Enormous Balloons, Ready to Lift*

Pirate Girl, still in her jeweled cape, tilts her head toward the sky and the circle of sun, heading toward the horizon. "It's nearly the golden hour of twilight," she says.

Jo, in her brocade gown, stands at the edge of the curve of light, not going forward yet, as if she's terribly worried about what she might find. "She's canceled it, I'm sure. This morning when I wasn't there. She would have given up by then."

"We'll find her, Jo," Pirate Girl says. "We'll tell her you're here. Maybe it's not too late."

So they emerge from the confusing and magical and frightening place that is the Wilds and step into the farthest corner of Huge Meadow. The perfect yellow light of this fading fall day turns everything such a beautiful shade of goldenness that it's almost hard to see, especially after the darkness of the Wilds. But when Henry's eyes adjust, he gasps.

"Oh!" Jo cries, and Button, in her green velvet collar, jumps around their knees, and Henry's chest fills with the kind of large feeling that makes it hard to speak. Because stretched out before them now, in the farthest, most safe and secret corner of Huge Meadow, is every possible part of a celebration, just waiting like a held breath—white tents, and flower garlands, and a fine cake of seven layers, and even a burbling fountain spilling Fizzé Joyeux. Henry sees a gathering of musicians, their instruments paused expectantly in their laps, and he sees the good people of the Timeless Province—the Dante family, with Rocco and Coco

226

and Otto wearing their best and finest clothes, and Ms. Esmé Silvooplay, and Sir Loinshank Jr. and Sir Loinshank Sr. both, and Rinaldo Francois, from La GreenWee, and Ms. Toomey, from Socket-Toomey Hardware, and so many more. He sees Jo's little sisters, Luna and Lola, with wreaths of flowers in their hair. And of course, he sees Jo's mother, Isabelle Idár, and Miss Becky in beautiful dresses, a trail of flowers woven into Miss Becky's long braid. But the good people wander about with their worried heads bent down solemnly, and the musicians' instruments are still and silent, and Jo's mother and Miss Becky sit close together, grasping hands in sorrow and anxiety.

"Go, Jo. Go!" Henry says, and she does. Jo begins to run, lifting the skirts of her brocade dress, her embroidered hat flying from her head. Pirate Girl cheers, and Apollo, in his green satin knee-pants and white shirt with puffed sleeves, hops up and down with joy.

"Mom! Mom!" Jo shouts, and what an incredible sight— Isabelle Idár's head turns at her daughter's voice, and so does Miss Becky's, and Jo's little sisters run to her and grab her around the waist. Isabelle Idár runs, too, and she's a swirl of white flying toward Jo, nearly lifting her off her feet as she smothers her with kisses. Henry is filled with such gladness that there are no words for it.

"Thank goodness! Thank goodness you're all right!" Isabelle Idár cries.

"I made it, Mom. I'm here! The celebration!"

"I kept believing," Jo's mother says, making Henry's throat tighten with emotion. "That you were all right. I kept hoping for this very moment, where my girl would run across this meadow."

Now, Mr. and Mrs. Dante, dressed in stylish attire and elaborate hats, rush over, and Henry is scooped up into a bundle of hugs and great relief and questions about where they have been and what has happened, though there is no time to answer all of this quite yet. Next, Ms. Fortune, who must have had some sort of unlucky calamity, hobbles over on a pair of crutches, her gown charming but quite long, and her hat lovely but somewhat dangerous.

*Somewhat Dangerous*

"We're so sorry, Ms. Fortune," Apollo says. "About . . ." He hooks his thumb over to Jason Scrum, already munching on the last leaves on the Huge Meadow trees.

"Never mind, we'll deal with him later," Ms. Fortune says.

"It's almost . . ." She looks at her wristwatch, which has apparently stopped. "Well, I have no idea."

"Almost the golden hour of twilight!" Pirate Girl exclaims. "It's time! It's time for the celebration of love to begin!"

And this is exactly what happens. The musicians begin to play a song that you *feel* even more than you hear. First, there are the long, pounding chords of an ancient organ, and then the ba-bamp rhythm of a drum and a bass, and then Isabelle Idár and Miss Becky join hands.

"Dearly beloved!" Isabelle Idár calls to the crowd. "We are gathered here today to get through this thing called life."

*"Together,"* Miss Becky says.

"Forever," Isabelle Idar says. "And that's a mighty long time."

Jo and Luna and Lola stand with them, too: a family. Henry's eyes overflow with tears. Apollo and Henry and Pirate Girl hold hands tightly, their hearts full, so full of the goodness of love, and those three most magic words, *I love you,* given rightly and joyously.

At this most beautiful of moments, when everyone gulps back tears and feels the purity and everlasting shine of connection, you may be hoping that the bully, Jason Scrum, will be transformed by what he's witnessing. But no. Sadly, he just keeps on being who he is, a selfish creature in his own world, munching whatever greenery he can find, oblivious to the important thing happening right in front of him.

But this doesn't matter a bit. Jo's mother and Miss Becky

raise their joined hands, and everyone cheers. Their eyes glint and glimmer with happiness, and they gather Jo and her sisters in their arms, and it's almost more than Henry can bear, because his chest is so full of joy. Apollo's eyes are wet behind his glasses, and Pirate Girl's cheeks are flushed, and Henry lifts Button into his arms to squeeze her with gratitude, and even Mr. Reese is snuffling, overcome, wiping his little squirrel eyes with the corner of his apron.

"It's . . ." Henry can't talk. His chest is full of emotion.

"Beautiful," Pirate Girl manages to say, squeezing Henry's hand.

Now, on that particular evening in fall, the season that is all about change, as the golden hour of twilight begins to darken, a magnificent party begins. The musicians pick up their instruments again—a bass, an electric guitar, drums, and horns, and out come the booming, shouting rhythms of celebration. Glasses are overflowing with Fizzé Joyeux. Rocco and Coco stick their thumbs in the second layer of the seven-layer cake and lick off the icing. Music works its own peculiar and particular magic. People begin to dance. Jo's mother and Miss Becky, of course, but also Mr. Dante and Coco, and Mrs. Dante and Rocco, and Jo and her little sisters, and Apollo and Pirate Girl and Henry and Button in a circle, as baby Otto toddles around, dancing solo. Dr. Frederick Valhalla, optometrist and man-about-town, gives

Miss Red from the bookstore a spin, and Sir Loinshank Sr. dips Ms. Fortune rather precariously, and Henry has to fling off his coat because it can get quite hot to whirl and shimmy in velvet. Mr. Reese has much better rhythm than you'd ever imagine. Ms. Esmé Silvooplay cuts loose with an unusual interpretive dance.

*An Unusual Interpretive Dance*

And the beat goes on.

Finally, night has fallen. In the darkness, strings of little white lights glow over the dance floors. Any doubt and mistrust of others that Vlad Luxor spread around their land have vanished. Surrounding the partygoers are the things that make every person similar and that we *all* experience—the sky we live beneath, the ground we all walk on, the wilds around us; love and friendship and growing up, struggles and seasons and music. Around them, too, are the things that make us different and singular. Henry thinks the sky is indigo, and Pirate Girl sees it as more bluish-black, and Apollo spots a shooting star, but Jo doesn't notice. Mr. and Mrs. Dante step on each other's shoes and bump into the table while dancing, spilling someone's drink, while Sir Loinshank Jr. and Rinaldo Francois waltz with the elegance of swans on a summer lake. Rocco taps his toes out of sync with the rhythm, and Coco wiggles her hips wildly, and Henry's elbows poke this way and that, and Ms. Toomey can't hear the beat at all, but she feels it in the soles of her feet, and one tree leans and whooshes this way, and another leans and whooshes that, but they are all, every one of them, still dancing.

Henry is dancing with all his might. His happiness fills him, and so does the heart-thump of the music, so much so that he doesn't even care if his thin legs look silly, or if his toe pokes from his shoe. He dances for all he's worth. And right then, because he's lost himself so completely in that music, he accidentally steps on the cord of the strings of lights. They flicker, and everyone gives a surprised *Ah!* and of course, this, *this* is when something astonishing happens. The gerenuk who is munching on a branch hanging just above the cake is—*pow!*—quite suddenly a boy on his toes who can't reach the limb.

"Hey! Wait a minute. Wait just one minute! I was enjoying that delicious treat!" Jason Scrum complains. But his gerenuk legs have vanished, just like that, and so have his horns, and his wide and alien-like eyes. Quite strangely, though, even from a bit of a distance, Henry can tell he is still quite smelly.

"What happened?" Henry shouts over the music.

*The spell!* Jo mouths, because these things are still dangerous to speak about loudly, even in the farthest and most hidden corner of Huge Meadow.

"Or, at least, *most* of it! Pee-yew!" Pirate Girl says.

"But how?" Apollo asks.

"I have no idea!" Jo shouts happily.

The Dantes notice, too, and begin hopping up and down with spell-breaking joy, and Mrs. Dante loses her hat, and Vic Chihuahua squashes it accidentally, but no one cares. The musicians do not skip a beat, adding to the merriment. Ms. Fortune hobbles toward Jason on her crutches and then hugs him so hard that they both tumble forward, her knees scraping the ground.

"Ow!" she cries in glee.

"Ow," Jason cries, in complaint.

"Thank you, children," Ms. Fortune cries. "Thank you!"

Henry and the others stand together, and Pirate Girl takes Henry's hand in one of hers, and then Jo's in the other, and Jo takes Apollo's. Button sits proudly next to Henry's knees.

"We did it," Jo says, "or, at least, I think so."

"Somehow we must have," Apollo says.

"It's just like the last time," Pirate Girl says. "When we

had to trust and go forward bravely, even though we didn't know all the hows and whats and whys."

"I guess it is," Henry says.

And while they don't entirely understand what has happened yet, and while they can see, or rather *smell*, that Jason has only *mostly* been returned to the way he was, in the farthest corner of Huge Meadow, at the hidden outer edge of the Wilds, with the music pulsing fabulously through him, Henry feels certain that a spell has indeed been broken.

CHAPTER 34

# A Silent, Loud Voice

"Where are you going, Henry Every?" Henry's mother yells, just before Henry reaches the front door. "You were gone for two days! Don't you know how worried we were that you'd never be back to do your chores?"

"Ugh, he's just like my father," Mr. Every says, turning up the television.

Oh, it is always so difficult to go from love and joy to nerve-racking anxiety and fear. But, *sigh*. This is the truth of Henry's life. His fine clothes are gone, and he's back in his thin jeans and too-small shirt and those tennis shoes that make his toes feel like sardines, squished in a tin.

Today, though, Henry and Button have somewhere they need to be. Somewhere very important.

"I asked you a question!

*Sardines, Squished in a Tin*

Where are you going?" Mrs. Every stands in front of the door, blocking their exit. When she speaks, Henry can see the big, scary cave of her open mouth.

"Oh, let him go. And that yippy-yappy nuisance of a dog. Our bad luck we got stuck with those two," Mr. Every says. "Be back before *never*," he snarls, still staring at the television.

"Fine! Leave me all alone, then!" Mrs. Every says. "Leave me here all by myself!"

Henry's stomach aches, but his hand reaches the door-knob. And he turns it oh so slowly, because when you live in a house like Henry's, *everything* is a version of a tiptoe. *Turrnn* . . . The knob clicks, and he eeeeases the door open ever so carefully.

It's almost wide enough for Henry and Button to escape. Almost. Then his mother says it. Then it happens. "Aren't you forgetting something, Henry Every?"

Fear scoots up his back like a shiver, and he feels a yucky something down deep. It's a feeling he can't entirely understand, let alone explain out loud, like those confusing words where some letters are silent. But what he does next . . . well, it's extraordinarily brave and even somewhat dangerous. Now, you may not appreciate just *how* brave and somewhat dangerous it is, not if you're allowed to sometimes ignore your parents or talk back or complain or whine or say no or even, heavens, shout or stomp your feet. Henry, of course, doesn't dare do any of those things, so when he and Button quickly scoot through the narrow space of the door without him saying those three most precious and magical words that his mother is waiting for, it is most definitely brave.

Henry's heart is pounding. He is trying not to hear the screech of HOW DARE YOU, HENRY EVERY. He moves as fast as he can before her arm can reach out to grab him by the neck. He runs down those steps, with Button at his heels, and while Henry is full of terror, he also feels a small, new something else. The beginnings of his own voice. It's not very loud—in fact, back there it was silent as a stone—but it could still be heard.

"Hurry, Henry!" Apollo shouts. All the children are on the sidewalk this morning, with their bikes that Mr. Dante retrieved from Hollow Valley. Apollo has Henry's bike upright and ready, and he jumps on.

"Let's get out of here," Jo says. Her hands grip her handlebars.

"Hop in, Button," Pirate Girl says as the dog scurries into Pirate Girl's sidecar.

"Come on, you guys!" Apollo makes sure his helmet is secure, and then takes off.

The foggy morning has that smoky smell of fall, and the drifting ribbons of white are eerie enough that the children imagine Needleman lurking behind every lamppost, even though, on this day, Mr. Reese is keeping an especially close watch. They hurry through town, past the billboard with the messages that always change but always stay the same, too: OTHERS AND ITS! A NATIONAL EMERGENCY! Then, they bump down onto the path across Huge Meadow, and pedal madly to the Circle of the Y, where one road leads up, up to Vlad Luxor's horrible tower on the mountain, and one road leads down to their shining destination.

When the road curves toward the lighthouse, and they are flying so fast that Henry barely has to pedal, that small, new *something else* feeling blooms in his chest. Henry did not give away those precious, magical three words, and for a few moments, he's filled with a glorious soaring, and the wind whips past his cheeks and through his hair. That morning, well, first he was afraid, he was petrified. But now he holds his head up high. In his whole body, he feels the deep bass beat of the strongest and most ancient and powerful things you can think of—the eye of a tiger, a dragon breathing fire, titanium.

And then he does something very *un*-Henry when no one is looking. He pumps his fist in the air in victory.

## CHAPTER 35
# The Details of *Bizarro Crueltildo*

The Beautiful Librarian has the large book of spells out on the library table, and Captain Every is leaning over it. The children have just told the two of them every gory and frightening and victorious detail of their adventure, from the trek through the weird Wilds, to the Shadow enemy who wasn't an enemy at all, to their own personal triumphs. Grandfather Every is tsk-tsking, and hmm-ing, and ah-ing as he reads the tiny words. Outside the lighthouse, the wind howls a bit, and under the table, Button is curled up on Henry's feet. It gives him that cozy warm feeling you might see on a holiday postcard.

*A Holiday Postcard*

"Well?" Pirate Girl asks. "Is it any clearer why Jason Scrum turned back into a boy but is still smelly like a gerenuk, even though he did not walk on the line between good and evil, falling on the side of good?" Which, we might point out, is quite an unwieldy thing to say.

"Oh!" Grandfather Every looks up. "My apologies! I was reading ahead to various *other* spells I am sure you will encounter."

"You weren't reading about *Bizarro Crueltildo*?" Apollo asks.

"Oh, no, no! No need. It's already abundantly clear why *that* happened, of course. Clear as your perfect vision in those fine spectacles."

Apollo smiles.

"Big. We should perhaps stick to the here and now. Show them the page," The Beautiful Librarian says. "The children are confused about the stinky bully."

"Ah. Yes. Quite right." Grandfather Every shuffles the pages of the big book, and then he points. "What happened to the bully . . . Yes. *Here.*"

"'*Bizarro Crueltildo*. Duration: somewhat permanent,'" Apollo reads.

"But that's the same page we saw before," Henry says.

"Well, yes. Of course it is! You attempted the more danger-ous spell-breaking option, number two: 'In a far corner of the world, walk the victim of *Bizarro Crueltildo* along the line between good and evil, falling to the side of good.' Which, as you know, most unfortunately failed. Jason Scrum fell to the side of evil, though, quite honestly, the line between good and evil is *always* hard to determine, let alone dangerous to walk along, which is perhaps why option two is strongly warned against. What you *succeeded* at was spellbreaking option number *one*: 'Accompany victim to a large gathering involving music, particularly stylish attire, and high spirits . . .'"

"The celebration of love," Jo says.

"Our fancy clothes," Apollo says.

"And as I mentioned before, if you read forward in this rather lengthy spell, you'll see that the next aim is to seek an unexpected outcome among flickering lights."

"The lights flickered when I stepped on the cord," Henry remembers.

"And that's when Jason Scrum turned back into a boy!" Pirate Girl realizes.

"I told you. Music has its own timeless and ever-present magic," Grandfather says, with great importance.

"I felt the magic that night!" Jo exclaims.

"But wait. Why is he still as stinky as a gerenuk?" Pirate Girl asks.

"Well, this *is* a mystery," Grandfather says. "Alas. I never did find out why Ms. Sumac stayed a Sparklemuffin. And I couldn't go back to reread those smudgy parts where I spilled the cologne." He sighs. Outside the lighthouse, the waves crash in and out again. The children feel the small ache of an unanswered question.

"Maybe I can help," The Beautiful Librarian says. She holds up a finger. "I'll be back in a moment."

Both Grandfather Every and Pirate Girl remove their pocket watches and click the little button at the top. Henry hears The Beautiful Librarian running up and down the library stairs, removing volumes and setting them back again, muttering things like "Maybe . . . no" and "Wait, perhaps . . ." until she finally says, "I've got it!" and dashes back to the table again.

Grandfather Every and Pirate Girl click their stopwatches again.

"Wow," Pirate Girl says. "That was almost a moment exactly."

"Quite extraordinary. A new record," Captain Every says.

The Beautiful Librarian hands the red leather book to Captain Every. "Thank heavens for multiple sources!" she says cheerfully.

Captain Every squinches his eyes and tilts his head. "*Tinsel, mcdoodle, crocodilius*? Ugh. I can't make out the words. It's atrocious, the way the print shrinks with each passing year! This is harder to read than a baffling sheet of music."

*A Baffling Sheet of Music*

"Let me sum up," The Beautiful Librarian says as they all lean in. She clears her throat. "Spell-breaking option one most certainly works, as you children discovered. Just not on adults, hence Mrs. Sumac remaining a Sparklemuffin. Once a bully has reached a certain age, they often stay a bully, and no amount of magic can change that unfortunate situation."

"Ah! So option one would *never* have worked on Mrs. Sumac! I must have read it too hastily in my great excitement to go to the disco. And then I knocked over the cologne, smudging the essential information. *I* was the glitch in the spell!" Grandfather admits with merriment. "But as you see, a plan *did* present itself, and I *did* follow it to great success, since Mrs. Sumac *was* transformed, only not in the way I expected."

"That's what happened to us, too!" Jo says. "It's just like you said, Pirate Girl. We trusted and went forward bravely, even though we didn't know the hows and whats and whys."

"As for young bullies and the spell duration as *somewhat permanent* . . . ," The Beautiful Librarian continues. "Well, some children *can* change, and others won't, and there's no telling who is who. Occasionally, in circumstances of extreme yuckiness, a . . . hmm, let's call it *a warning*. A small warning is built into the spell, leaving something quite noticeable that cannot be entirely undone."

"A warning? Like the warning stink the caribou gave off?" Jo asks.

"Yes," The Beautiful Librarian says. "But in that case, they were warning each other, and in this case, the warning is to everyone else."

"How handy!" Pirate Girl says. "I wish every bully came with a warning."

"Will he have it forever?" Jo asks.

"It's hard to say. He *was* cruel about love, and that's exceptionally awful. All we can do is hope that he will learn to do better so the stink can wear off in time," she says.

"Do you think he ever will?" Henry asks.

"It's hard to know," The Beautiful Librarian says. "Sometimes, cruelty is like a very strong cologne. A person stops smelling it on themselves. Other times, though, a person will tire of seeing everyone else crinkle their nose whenever they walk into a room. And then they decide to change."

CHAPTER 36

# A Spell-Breaking Feast

B ack in Captain Every's dining room now, the children and Captain Every and The Beautiful Librarian and Button indulge in a great celebratory feast, including an aromatic tower of Jelled Noodle, and a Frankfurter Crown, and a stunning bowl of golden Egg Vrouvret. Warm buttered rolls, tricolored jam. Asparagus à la Glutton. Fronds of Beef. Garbanzo Galactic in lime and berry. Glasses filled to the brim with a perfectly aged bottle of Boublé Milk Magnifico, a gift from Mrs. Sumac years ago.

In his tummy, Jelled Noodle swims like an eel, and Henry is sure he can't eat another bite. Until they move to the living room, that is, where, on the coffee table, he sees the tray of five astonishing cakes.

Pirate Girl chooses cakes one and three, and Apollo chooses cakes two, three, and four, and The Beautiful Librarian takes a slice of each. Henry decides on cakes one, two, three, and four, and after that, he is utterly and

*Five Astonishing Cakes*

wonderfully stuffed. Still, even after licking the last bit of cocoa-coconut frosting from his fork, something is troubling Henry.

"Grandfather?" He hates to even ask. He doesn't want to spoil the mood, but he needs to know.

"Yes, son?"

"Was it . . . all for nothing?" he asks. "The trip through the Wilds, the cave, the Forest of Knives? Our fright with the Shadow? Being captured by Needleman and locked in the lodge? Our narrow escape, thanks to the caribou?"

"I was wondering the same thing," Pirate Girl says softly. "I mean, we could have just taken Jason Scrum to the celebration."

"The Forest of Knives was terrifying." Apollo licks his fork.

"And we almost didn't make the celebration at all," Jo says, sipping another glass of Boublé Milk.

"*Of course* it wasn't all for nothing! Absolutely and

unequivocally not!" Grandfather booms, his cheeks turning a jovial red. "What if we *always* knew the easiest road and took it every time? How would we learn *anything*? How would we stumble upon the surprising glow of nature or the view from unexpected heights?"

"But we didn't just see glowworms. Bad stuff happened, too," Apollo says.

"Dear children, of course it did! The whole, messy, tumbling story is important! Good *and* bad. Each ticking minute of the clock leading to each hour of past and present. The start and the finish. The trials and tribulations before the triumphs. The frights, the shudders, the eye-opening realizations! And we can *never* entirely know the hows and whats and *especially* the whys of *any* adventure, until we *have* the adventure." Grandfather Every beams first at Pirate Girl, and then at each of them. "Magic is mystery! Mystery is magic! This entire spell was *essential*. Certainly not trivial and most definitely part of the *larger* story."

"But I don't feel like I actually did anything, not like a *real* spell breaker. More like it just happened," Apollo says.

"Didn't *do* anything? You, Apollo Dante, from your long line of great thinkers and philosophers, gatherers of knowledge for greater understanding—you brought your own specific weirdness to that perilous journey through the Wilds. What would have happened to all of you without the information you gained by always *having your nose in a book*, as the bully said? And you used your fine spectacles to spot shelter and danger, and to signal for help. *Spell breaker,*" Grandfather says.

Apollo beams. "I guess I did."

Now Grandfather turns to Pirate Girl. "And you, Carson Curie Shackleton, otherwise known as Pirate Girl, descendant of fearless explorers and scientists, brave wayfarers who keep going forward when others stop . . . Why, I shudder to think what might have happened without *your* specific weirdness. Your unusual spirit and courage, and the contents of your pockets, and the pocketknife you carry everywhere, noted specifically by the bully . . . For starters, you'd all still be tied up in rope, and so would Jason Scrum himself. *Spell breaker,*" he says.

"Maybe you're right," Pirate Girl says, and smiles.

"And Josephine Idár. From a long line of people who have fought for justice and looked after the less fortunate—under extremely stressful personal circumstances, your weirdness gave you the strength and determination of a leader in battle. You thought of others before yourself when your troop needed rest. And your fine and accurate mathematical calculations allowed Henry to ace the landing out the window. He could have broken his neck, so thank you. *Spell breaker,*" Grandfather Every says to Jo.

"And let's not forget the celebration of love," The Beautiful Librarian says. "Love made fun of, ugh, by a bully! The celebration helped break the spell, *and* it brought joy to many people in the province. For the first time since you-know-who started going on and on about *others*—there was a feeling of togetherness. It was also a wild party they'll remember for years! We would have been there ourselves, but the light-house weather system had wrongly predicted a storm, and Big had just made me an irresistible Aphrodite Ambrosia." The Beautiful Librarian, keeper of the knowledge, winks at Grandfather Every, keeper of the light, and he winks back.

"The day of the party was the happiest one of my life so far," Jo says.

"And you, Henry," Grandfather says, taking his hand. "You, who must listen and watch so closely out of fear, you, who are sometimes too afraid to go to sleep—you were extraordinarily brave, even when you were terrified. You reached your hand out to Apollo up on that ledge. You dodged Needleman's knife as adeptly as a ball at recess. You, with your beautiful weirdness, you fit through that window perfectly, and made the narrowest and most coura-geous rescue, all by yourself. *Spell breaker.*"

Henry feels so proud, he could cry. His throat tightens. His eyes begin to water.

"But more than that, Henry . . . more than *that*—you, who so often feel sad, and bad, and alone . . . you still took love and beauty and music into your heart, and *you danced.*"

## CHAPTER 37

# The Spinning Circle

I hate to tell them the bad news after this glorious feast," The Beautiful Librarian says. She has a smudge of Vanilla Madam-Missure cake on her nose.

"Ah, I know," Captain Every agrees. "Why, oh, why is cruelty so timeless?"

"I have no idea," she says as Button snags a fallen piece of Shimmer Torte from the rug and wolfs it down in one bite.

"What bad news?" Pirate Girl is the only one brave enough to ask.

"Vlad Luxor," Captain Every says, in quite a loud and strong voice, not only because he's the senior-most spell breaker, but because the lighthouse is a place of safety, with a revolving beam that never dims in any darkness or storm. "The wall, the wall, the wall!"

"But there is no wall," Henry says.

"It was only a piece of string," Apollo says.

"He couldn't seem to build one even with all the magic and power in the world," Pirate Girl says.

"Oh, but, children, I'm afraid you're wrong," Grandfather says. "He has certainly built a wall. One that's much more dangerous than any actual structure of bricks or stone. A wall between people! A wall between inners and outers, and it's getting higher and more treacherous every day. The evil is getting worse and uglier by the second, and spreading like a rash. You *must* stop him."

"I don't know how we could ever stop him," Henry says. "I could barely even *look* at him."

"I was shaking in my boots whenever he was near us," Pirate Girl says, although Henry couldn't tell.

"I had a hard time dealing with a gerenuk bully, let alone one as bad as he is," Jo says.

"Same here," Apollo says.

"Shaking in your boots will be the least of it," The Beautiful Librarian adds. "When you're finally ready."

"Finally ready?" Henry says, and shivers. This whole conversation is quite nerve-racking. Apollo's eyes are wide behind his glasses. Pirate Girl leans forward.

"You have more to learn, of course, before taking on something *that* large," The Beautiful Librarian says.

"More to learn?" Pirate Girl asks. "But how?"

Grandfather Every laughs. "*How?* Spell breaking, of course! I told you, did I not, that one needs the whole experience, good and bad, before you understand the *whys*? Well, here is your *why*," Grandfather says, sticking his fork straight into a cake and taking a bite. "That stinky, troublesome bully—did you think *he* was the important part of *this* adventure? A spell is as much for the spell breaker as a spell breaker is for the spell. And you, my weird, beautiful darlings, had some very important things to learn, especially in this time of *outers* and *others*."

"What do you mean?" Pirate Girl asks.

"He means that if you're going to fight an evil bully who wants to divide us all with walls, there are vital truths to understand, about other people and about yourselves and your own powers and strengths," The Beautiful Librarian says.

"What truths?" Apollo asks.

"One." Captain Every holds up a single, sure finger. "That there are evil individuals like Vlad Luxor and Needleman, and even like your parents, Henry. But there are also just shadows."

"Jenny." Pirate Girl smiles.

"And, two," The Beautiful Librarian continues, "that *weird* is the most natural and necessary and valuable thing on earth, thankfully present in every plant, animal, and human. A gift. A *force*. *Otherness* is essential to the varied beauty of life on this planet."

*The Varied Beauty of*
*Life on This Planet*

"The monkey pitcher." Jo giggles.

"The glowworms," Henry remembers.

"Caribou knees, and painted trees," Apollo says, making a poem and not even realizing it.

*"Me,"* Pirate Girl says.

*"All* of us," Henry says, and the others nod.

"Big, look! They understand! This is some of the most excellent and successful spell breaking I have ever seen." The Beautiful Librarian clasps her hands in joy.

"Oh, it is." Captain Every beams. "The bully may still stink like an old egg, but the children have definitely been changed!"

"Did *you* learn something with each spell, Captain Every?" Apollo asks. "Did you learn something after Ms. Sumac, even though the spell wasn't broken?"

"Oh, the spell was most certainly broken! Her new uniqueness was extraordinary! Before that, she was just a regular old bully. And I most definitely learned something about myself, as well. I always thought I had two left feet, but it turns out I can shake my groove thing rather adeptly."

"Shake your groove thing, Captain Every?" Jo asks.

"An old-fashioned way of saying he's quite a good dancer," The Beautiful Librarian says.

"Which reminds me, my darling, of all the *other* things that are timeless besides cruelty. Things that bring us together, not apart. An important and ever-present one, rare in that everyone on earth shares *this* in common, no matter what particular sort it is."

"Hmm," The Beautiful Librarian says. "I believe you're referring to that thing that sneaks into our smallest moments and fills them with meaning. That lets us all be weird and free and ourselves. The heartbeat, bass beat, ba-bump of all our lives."

"I am indeed. Shall we put on a record?"

"A record, Captain Every?" Pirate Girl asks.

"A large round disc that plays music," The Beautiful Librarian explains. "That's a wonderful idea, Big."

*A Large Round Disc That Plays Music*

Grandfather Every hops up and sets one of those large discs onto a spinning circle, and he turns the volume up, and the room fills with a thundering thumping beat. "Come here, my darling," he shouts over the music, reaching out to take The Beautiful Librarian's hand. "Ah, ah, ah, ah, staying alive, staying alive!" he sings. He sings so loud, Henry can see his tonsils.

And now Henry hops up, too, and so do Apollo and Jo and Pirate Girl, and they all start dancing together, and this causes Button to get so excited she starts barking and running in circles, and the room is practically shaking with sound, the walls pulsing, full of noisy life. They are wiggling their shoulders, and sloshing their hips around like ships at sea. Henry feels so, so happy. He can't think about anything other than what's happening at this very minute. His grandfather lifts him right up off his feet, and his legs dangle down.

"I love you, Grandfather!" he shouts into the music.

"I love you, Henry. I love you, my boy!" Grandfather shouts in return, and then has to set him down, because he may have twinged his back.

The music goes on.

If you were there in that room, you would be stomping and spinning and feeling ah, ah, ah, ah alive. Around you, the walls would be shaking and the floor thumping. You would wipe the sweat from your forehead. You would reach for another slice of Shimmer Torte and another glass of Boublé Milk Magnifico so that you could keep dancing.

But you are here instead, wherever that is. Wondering about all the things that will happen next, and all the things that haven't yet been answered, because of course the story continues, even if this page ends. What terrifying but glorious adventure will the children have next? What about Mr. Reese? Will he always be a caring but bad-tempered rodent in a dress? Does Needleman finally catch them, as he surely might? How will the children ever defeat Vlad Luxor, especially when his evil keeps getting worse and worse? What awful thing is going to happen to Apollo? And is that all we'll hear about Brenda and Eddie? Nothing more than we've been told already?

Well, these are just a few of the things we don't yet know. There is so much more, every year and second and moment of the future. And what is happening in that house by the sea—maybe it's in the future, too, or maybe in the past, or maybe tomorrow or yesterday, who can say.

Do this, though. Do this most important thing: Zoom in to that lit window, zoom in to that room, until *right this minute* you can feel the beat of the music in your heart. And then: Zoom out. Watch the golden glow of that place get farther and farther away, until you can't even see it anymore, until the glow is only a memory. Let that be in your heart, too.

# Acknowledgments

Big, giant love and boundless thanks to Jen Klonsky and Michael Bourret. I am so lucky, lucky, lucky to have these two in my corner as my editor, as my agent, and as my *friends*. Gratitude again to our incredible design team: Theresa Evangelista, Tony Sahara, Patrick Faricy (oh, that amazing cover art!), and Adam Nickel (our mapmaker!). To the entire team—thank you: Laurel Robinson, Jacqueline Hornberger, Cindy Howle, Caitlin Tutterow, Vanessa DeJesus, Carmela Iaria, Trevor Ingerson, Venessa Carson, Summer Ogata, and our whole sales crew.

A shout-out of love to John Cardinali and Rock Hushka, two of my favorite people in the world. Forever appreciation to Paul and Jan Caletti, Evie Caletti, and Sue Rath, too. Sam and Nick—I am grateful for you, Erin, Pat, Myla, and Max every single day. Vast and infinite love to you guys. And, John Yurich—you're the partner and friend I always wished and wished for. *Beloved* is the one, right word.

## About the Author

**Deb Caletti** lives in a far north corner of the world. She is frightened of squirrels, owns a splendid pocketknife, and writes on an Underwood Standard Typewriter, 14 inch.

*Underwood Standard Typewriter, 14 Inch*